Movie Star Down!

"There he is—Justin Carraway. Told you it would be easy finding a movie star in Bayport," Joe said. He rubbed his hands together. "Time to work my mojo."

Justin stood about half a block away, talking to a thin girl with blond hair. "You're telling me that this famous mojo of yours can work from this distance?" I asked.

"It's a powerful thing," Joe answered. "But I'll probably have to get a tiny bit closer," he admitted after a beat.

"I really think this is a situation that cries out for a plan B," I said.

Justin kissed the blond girl. Then he turned and started walking toward us.

"Plan A is going to work just fine," Joe retorted.

Then the sound of a gunshot rang out.

And Justin Carraway went down.

THE HARDY BOYS

Undercover Brothers®

Available from Simon & Schuster

THE HARDY BOYS

Undercover Brothers®

FRANKLIN W. DIXON

#25 Double Trouble

Aladdin Paperbacks
New York   London   Toronto   Sydney

If you purchased this book without a cover, you should be aware that this book is stolen property. It was reported as "unsold and destroyed" to the publisher, and neither the author nor the publisher has received any payment for this "stripped book."

This book is a work of fiction. Any references to historical events, real people, or real locales are used fictitiously. Other names, characters, places, and incidents are the product of the author's imagination, and any resemblance to actual events or locales or persons, living or dead, is entirely coincidental.

ALADDIN PAPERBACKS
An imprint of Simon & Schuster Children's Publishing Division
1230 Avenue of the Americas, New York, NY 10020
Copyright © 2008 by Simon & Schuster, Inc.
All rights reserved, including the right of reproduction in whole or in part in any form.
THE HARDY BOYS MYSTERY STORIES, HARDY BOYS UNDER-COVER BROTHERS, ALADDIN PAPERBACKS and related logo are registered trademarks of Simon & Schuster, Inc.
Designed by Sammy Yuen Jr.
The text of this book was set in Aldine 401 BT.
Manufactured in the United States of America
First Aladdin Paperbacks edition November 2008
10 9 8 7 6 5 4 3 2 1
Library of Congress Control Number 2008920167
ISBN-13: 978-1-4169-6765-1
ISBN-10: 1-4169-6765-6

TABLE OF CONTENTS

JOE

1

Mission Accomplished

I could hear Bucky whinnying at me impatiently. "I'm coming, I'm coming," I muttered as I ran toward the horse. I untied him from the stump where my brother, Frank, had left him for me, then mounted up as fast as I could.

Bucky gave a little hop as I slid into the saddle. Horses don't get named Bucky for nothing. I urged him forward with my heels and we were off. Somewhere up ahead, Frank was running. We were in the middle of an all-teen Ride 'n Tie race.

Frank, Bucky, and I had already relayed our way more than twenty miles. Good thing ATAC agents have to stay in shape.

ATAC—that's American Teens Against Crime—

had assigned us the mission of finding a saboteur. At the last Ride 'n Tie, the course had been sabotaged. A horse had ended up badly injured. And its rider had ended up dead. ATAC had reason to believe this racecourse would be sabotaged too.

So far, nothing.

I stayed on alert as Bucky trotted down the path through the woods. A Ride 'n Tie is all about endurance—for the horses and the humans. Anyone who gallops—or sprints—is going to end up losing. There were fifty more miles of trail to go. Horses and runners were spread out all along the course.

We rounded a corner—and Bucky reared. I almost slid off of him.

"Whoa! Easy!" I cried. But Bucky was freaked. He reared again, letting out a high, panicked whinny. I scanned the area, trying to figure out what was causing Bucky's agitation.

Rattlesnake! Right on the path in front of us. Its head was arched up in strike position, the rattle on its tail shaking out a warning.

I twisted around and managed to pull a can of energy drink out of the saddlebag. It wasn't that heavy, but I thought it might be heavy enough. I took aim and hurled the can at the snake.

The motion scared Bucky as much as the snake did. He hopped sideways to the right in a move I didn't even know a horse could make. Then he reared up again, so high I thought he would topple backward.

He didn't.

But I did.

I landed in the dirt with a thud. Snake! Where was the snake?

And then I spotted it—just a few feet away from me. Lying motionless. I'd killed it. I picked it up and hurled it off the path. "It's gone, Bucky, okay. It's gone." He stomped his front hooves. His eyes rolled, showing white at the edges. "It's gone," I said again. Then I reached out and managed to snag Bucky's reins.

I walked him in a circle, giving him time to calm down. "Ready to go on?" I asked. Bucky snorted. I took that as a not-quite-yet and walked him in another circle. That's when I noticed the sun spark off something metallic a few feet away, not far off the trail.

I tied Bucky to the nearest tree, then headed over to check it out. I found a metal cage, about the size to hold a rabbit. But there wasn't a bunny inside. There were three more rattlers. And the cage door—it was open.

I broke a small branch off one of the trees and used it to shut the door. Then I studied the area. Yeah, there it was. I knew there'd be evidence. On the trunk of the tree I'd broken the branch off was a smear of greasepaint. A mix of purple and pink.

At the start of the Ride 'n Tie, all the horses were tied at the far end of a meadow. A lot of racers marked up their horses with greasepaint or tied bright ribbons on them to make them easier to pick out at a distance.

Only one person had used pink and purple paint. I knew who the saboteur was.

I headed back toward Bucky, making a lot of noise so any other snakes that had escaped from the cage knew to get out of the way.

"The rules are changing a little bit, Bucky," I told him as I untied his reins from the tree. I climbed into the saddle. "Now we're going to go fast. Let's see what you can do." I tapped my heels into his sides a couple of times and we were off. Galloping down the trail.

I leaned forward, keeping close to Bucky's body.

"Frank!" I shouted when I spotted my brother up ahead. He stopped jogging and turned back. "We've got sabotage. And I know who did it." I brought Bucky to a stop, and Frank leaped up on the saddle behind me.

"Okay, Bucky, mush!" I cried, giving the reins a shake. And Bucky mushed good. Dust flew up off the trail as he galloped.

I saw a horse and rider up ahead. Not the horse—or rider—I was looking for. I pulled the reins to the left and we galloped past.

"You're never going to make it to the end like that!" the rider shouted after us.

I didn't care about making it to the end. I just wanted to make it to the horse with the wild pink and purple flowers painted on its flank.

Bucky gave another whinny. And it wasn't the "hurry up" whinny. Or the "I'm scared out of my gourd" one. Nope, this was the happy, excited "I'm gonna see my girlfriend" sound.

"Get ready to rock and roll," I told Frank.

"I don't see anyone," he answered.

"You will," I said. I didn't need to urge Bucky to pick up speed. His girlfriend was up there, and that's where he wanted to be.

He sped around a curve in the trail. And, yep, there was Amber, Bucky's special lady with the pink and purple flowers on her hip. Ridden by Lisa, the saboteur. It didn't take us long to catch up to them. Amber was trotting and Bucky was galloping. At least until he reached her; then he slowed down to match her pace.

"Uh, hi," Lisa said. "You know it's cheating for both of you to be riding at once."

"Huh, I didn't think you'd be such a rule follower,"

I commented. "Since you left that cage full of rattle-snakes next to the trail."

Lisa didn't answer. Instead she dug her heels into Amber's side, and they took off at a gallop.

Bucky wasn't having that. He started galloping after them. He reached his girlfriend's side in seconds.

"Get as close as you can," Frank shouted.

Bucky was fine with close. My leg was almost bumping into Lisa's.

That's when Frank made his move. One second he was sitting behind me. Next he was behind Lisa, reaching around her to take the reins and signal Amber to stop.

Bucky stopped too. He gave Amber's muzzle a nuzzle. He was a happy boy. Frank and I were happy boys too. Mission accomplished.

FRANK

2

The Two Lives of Frank Hardy

Yesterday I was leaping onto the back of a galloping horse. Today I'm back in school, listening to Mr. Edwards talk about the gold standard. Sometimes being an agent with American Teens Against Crime gives me mental whiplash. Not that I'd give it up. Helping put away the assorted murderers, thieves, and arsonists makes me feel like I'm contributing to the world. Giving something back.

And it's something Joe and I can do that adults can't. ATAC sends us on missions where an adult would be out of place—like the teen Ride 'n Tie. No one over eighteen could have entered. The idea for using teens as operatives came from our dad. After he retired—he was a PI who did a lot of work for the police—he set up ATAC. Joe and I were the first recruits.

ATAC is one of the ways Dad has given something back.

 JOE

The other brother here. Okay, just wanted to say giving back, contributing, that's all good. But what Frank's not saying is that being with ATAC rocks. Kayaking, skiing, rappelling, flying, horseback riding— we do it all on our missions. It's like an extreme sport amusement park.

FRANK

Out, Joe. I'm telling this part. And, by the way, at that extreme sport amusement park my brother was talking about—he forgot to mention that a lot of times between rides, someone is trying to kill either you or a person you're supposed to be protecting.

Anyway. As I was saying, I was sitting in history, feeling like I'd jumped between parallel universes once too often. The door swung open, and Mr. Edwards looked annoyed. A lot of teachers chill out near the end of the school year. They give you assignments like crossword puzzles, and everybody— teachers included—spaces out a little, thinking about summer vacation. Not Mr. Edwards.

"What now?" he asked. "I'm trying to stuff a few key facts into these heads while I still have the chance."

I followed his gaze. Two girls had stepped into the room. I wasn't sure of their names, but I thought they were both freshmen. They were dressed up like Cupid. Sort of. The little gold bows and arrows, and the wings, and maybe the armloads of flowers were your usual Cupid stuff. The shiny red shorts, pink T-shirts, and pink sneaks, not so much.

"We're here to pass out bouquets," the taller Cupid explained to Mr. Edwards. "It's a fund-raiser for the band for next year. Remember, people placed orders to send flowers to their sweeties—today is the delivery date."

Mr. Edwards rolled his eyes. "Make it quick."

"Shouldn't take long," Brian Conrad commented. "Just hand them all over to me."

Murderers are the kind of bad I deal with in that other universe I was talking about. Brian Conrad is the bad in this one. He's not exactly dangerous. But he's one of those long-on-talk, short-on-action bullies who supply much of the unpleasantness around school.

"What's your name?" the shorter Cupid asked Brian. My friend Chet Morton snickered at the question. It was typical of Brian to just assume everyone knew who he was. A legend in his own mind, to use one of my aunt Trudy's favorite expressions.

"Uh, there might be one for you," the taller Cupid told Brian when he answered. She and the other girl flipped through the tags on the bouquets they held. "Yeah. Here you go." She handed him about five daisies tied together with a yellow ribbon.

"Your girlfriend went all out. She must have saved up for, what, at least a couple days to afford that," Greg Rhomer joked.

"Let's see what you got," Brian shot back.

"I want to know who that massive one is for," a girl who sat behind me called out.

"Okay." The taller Cupid looked at the tag on a bunch of what had to be two dozen red roses. "The lucky sweetie is—Frank Hardy."

I started to raise my hand, but she was already coming toward me. Brian snorted. "He sent them to himself," he muttered. Loudly.

"I'm betting on your sister," Greg commented to Brian. "She's always staring at him."

I hoped no one was staring at me right then. Because I felt a blush starting to creep up my neck, heading for my face. I took a deep breath, willing it away.

"Awww, he's blushing," Andrew Peterson, another

one of my so-called friends, pointed out.

Why did I even try? You can't control the involuntary nervous system by force of will. It's just not biologically possible.

"No way did Belinda send them," Brian snapped. "If she's always staring at him, it's because he's so repulsive." In case you hadn't noticed, Brian has only reached the fourth-grade level in comebacks.

I suspected the flowers might actually be from his sister. At least Joe was always saying she had a crush on me. I'm not sure. I'm not great at knowing what girls are thinking. I don't have very good girldar. I guess it's because I sort of avoid them. I hate blushing, and being around a cute girl—that pretty much always brings one on. There was this one girl once who I actually felt okay around. Comfortable. But it didn't exactly work out. Probably because Joe and I were the ones who proved she was a murderer.

"Give it up, Frank," Chet called as the Cupids handed out some more bouquets. "Who's it from?"

I shifted the bouquet, searching for the tag. Then I felt something rock solid. Something that definitely didn't belong in a bunch of flowers.

I tightened my grip on them. I didn't want anybody to see what had actually been delivered to me in the middle of history class.

Go Time

"**B**ring the player. Usual place."

I turned my head and saw Frank walking away down the hall. He had a bunch of roses in one hand. I don't get it. I am, objectively, the cuter Hardy. I've got the blond hair and the blue eyes. Everyone knows that's the best combo. I'm also a lot more fun than Frank. And I can hold a conversation with a girl without stammering and turning red. But did I get flowers? Well, yeah, actually. I got a couple of carnations from Madison Brownlee. But she's class president, and she gave flowers to everybody.

I shoved my books in my locker, grabbed my lunch and my game player, and slammed the door.

Then I headed toward the out-of-order bathroom with the not-pleasant smell. It's our favorite place to eat.

Psych. It's one of the places at school that's safe to watch one of the cartridges from ATAC. That's how we receive our missions—on what look like game cartridges. We only get to watch them once, so we have to remember everything the first time we see them. If you try to play them a second time, all you get is music. Usually something you really don't want anyone to hear you listening to. NKOTB, anyone? Didn't think so.

I knew Frank had received a cartridge. The request for the game player meant it was go time. We were about to find out what our next mission was.

"You really shouldn't have gotten me flowers," I told my brother as I stepped into the bathroom. "It's not my birthday or anything."

"My pleasure." He tossed the bouquet to me and held out his hand for the game player. "I wish ATAC had delivered them—and the cartridge—to you."

I laughed. "Yeah, it would have been so humiliating for everyone to think some girl liked me enough to spring for a multitude of roses."

Frank didn't answer. He has this policy of ignoring me when he doesn't like what I have to say. He snapped the cartridge in place. I moved closer, so I had a good view of the small screen.

A teenage guy ran up the side of a building. Right up the side of a building. "Cool. I am *so* going to see that movie the first day."

"What movie?" Frank asked.

"The new Justin Carraway one. *Z Force*," I told him. "The commercials for it are on practically every half hour." Frank still looked blank. "But I guess not on the Discovery Channel," I added.

"I don't get why you like his movies. I saw two of them, and they were both totally unrealistic. The laws of physics weren't even in play," said Frank.

"Who cares? His movies are slammin'," I said, my eyes locked on the game player's screen. I was hoping for a few seconds that were new. But the movie clip slid away, and Sanders Smith, the host of *Star Gazer*, slid on.

"Justin Carraway must have kept some of the superpowers he used in *Z Force*," Sanders said in his smooth announcer voice. "Look at what he was able to do to this hotel room in less than twelve hours."

The image of a completely totaled hotel room appeared behind Sanders's big head. Ever notice how people who make it famous on TV or in movies seem to have especially big heads? And often teeny little bodies. They are mutants. Evolutionarily, all humans should be wearing the big head, teeny body combo in a couple of thousand years.

"That's what your bedroom would look like if Aunt Trudy didn't stay on your case," Frank commented.

"Come on. I don't smash stuff up. Or tear the stuffing out of furniture. Or pull lighting fixtures out of the wall. I just like to have my stuff in easy reach. And sometimes easy reach is on the floor."

"Yeah, I can see why you'd never want to be more than an arm's length away from that moldy bologna sandwich I saw in there the other day," Frank answered.

Big-head Sanders's voice cut back in. "That's one more on the list of places that have banned Justin. It was just last week that the Ivy, one of L.A.'s power restaurants, asked him not to return. Justin set fire to the place, or at least acted like he was about to—it turned out he was just punking Rick Ortiz, one of his entourage." A clip of Justin laughing at a guy I assumed was Rick appeared on the screen; then there was another close-up of Sanders.

"And as of last night—you're never going to believe this—Justin was banned from a whole city," he said. "New Haven, Connecticut, voted to veto the permits necessary for Justin and company to film scenes on one of their main streets. Congrats,

Justin. Banned from an entire city at seventeen. Impressive."

Sanders leaned forward and lowered his voice. "I've got a suggestion for you, Justin. Next time you get in trouble, just whip this out." A new picture appeared behind Sanders. Justin at probably age four. "Who could resist that face, am I right?" Sanders continued.

He looked over his shoulder at the photo. "Actually, that could be Justin's twin brother, Ryan. Ryan used to be an actor too. He and Justin shared the part of little Jimmy O'Hara on *Five Times Five*. But it seems as if Ryan grew out of his talent. He gave up the biz when he turned eleven. Now he has a solid career as a member of big brother's posse. Fact of the night: Justin is older by a margin of only twenty-three minutes. And here's a bonus. A *Star Gazer* exclusive. The new location for Justin's movie is—Bayport."

"Whoa. You think maybe we could be extras or something?" I asked Frank. "That would be sweet."

"I think we're going to be busy. You know, with our *mission*," he said.

"Oh, right." I shouldn't admit this. But I'd forgotten for a second that I was supposed to be prepping for an ATAC assignment.

The screen went blank. *Star Gazer*'s hyper-peppy go-to-commercial music went silent.

A note on a piece of plain white paper filled the screen.

"Nothing unusual about the font. It's on every computer," Frank commented.

"Bet the paper is standard too," I said as I began to read the note. It said: *You think you're so special. And you've got everyone else believing it too. But if you get cut, I'm betting you bleed just like the rest of us.*

The note was quickly replaced by another one. This one was written on a sheet of pale lavender paper with flower petals glued to it. The edges of the petals had turned brown. It was a little harder to read than the first one, because the handwriting was really curly and loopy. My third-grade teacher would disapprove. According to her, cursive letters were supposed to look one way, and one way only. If anyone deviated from the system, we would no longer be able to communicate with one another in writing, and society as a whole would crumble.

Frank started reading the second note aloud— slowly. He was clearly having some problems with the handwriting too. " 'Justin, my love. We are meant to be together. I had both our charts done by an astrologist, and we are soul mates. There's no doubt it's our destiny to share our lives. What do I have to do to prove it to you? I'll do anything to make you see the truth. Maybe I'll have to kidnap you (ha, ha). That way you could spend enough time with me to really know me. Then you'd have to see the truth. I promise I'll find a way for us to see each other soon. Love, love, love, from your love.' "

"I'm not sure I believe the 'ha, ha' in that letter," I said.

"I definitely didn't think there was anything funny in it," Frank agreed, as another letter filled the screen. This one was on lined binder paper. Written all in caps, perfectly neat and uniform. But whoever had written the letter had pushed down so hard on the pen that it had made tears in a couple of places. The message was short and to the point: "Stop what you're doing—or you will be forced to stop."

The note stayed on the screen, as our ATAC contact began to speak. *"Justin Carraway receives thousands of letters a week. Many are harmless fan letters. But in the past month, the number of letters red-flagged as potentially threatening to Justin have increased. His manager, John 'Slick' Slickstein, has become concerned that the writer of one of these letters will go further and try to get in touch with Justin in person. Your mission is to get close to Justin yourselves, become a part of his entourage, and determine if he is in danger."*

The screen went blank. That was all the information we were going to get. The rest was up to us.

"I see psycho stalker possibilities in all those letters," I commented.

"And all of them contained a threat, or at least implied a threat," Frank pointed out. "One talked about cutting and blood. One writer came right out and said she wanted to kidnap Justin. And one claims he will stop Justin from doing what he's doing—although what that means, we don't know—if he doesn't stop on his own. So we've got three people who could possibly want to hurt Justin."

"The three letters were just samples," I reminded him. "Who knows how many other threats Justin has gotten? We might end up having to protect him from a whole army of stalkers."

Plan A

Joe handed me a baseball bat and pointed to the ceramic clown on his floor. "Smash it!" he ordered.

I let the bat hang at my side. "This isn't necessary," I protested.

"You're the one who's all about preparation," Joe reminded me. "Not just for cases, either. Don't think I don't know about your class-by-class checklist."

"That's only during exams," I said. "And I think if a situation comes up where I need to take care of a very ugly ceramic clown, I'll be up for it without a rehearsal."

"You won't. I know you," Joe insisted. "And

you're not going to make it as a member of Justin's entourage if you can't produce a little mayhem. If he wants to trash a motel room, you're going to have to do more than leave a towel on the bathroom floor. You're going to have to smash it up. So smash!" He pointed to the clown again.

Sometimes I just ignore Joe when he's being ridiculous. But sometimes he just won't be ignored. So I raised the baseball bat, aimed, and whacked the clown a good one.

A second later Aunt Trudy threw open the door and rushed inside. "What was that horrible noise?" she cried. Her eyes went from the bat in my hand to the pieces of clown and back to the bat. "Frank Hardy, why in the world would you do a thing like that? That was a present to Joe from Mrs. Iburg. She gave it to him when he was five years old. And she gave you a ceramic pirate. How would you like it if Joe destroyed your pirate?"

"He already did," I answered.

"When I was seven. And it was an accident," Joe protested.

"It was not," I shot back. "You hated it. You said it was always staring at you."

"Maybe I did give it a little help off your dresser," Joe admitted. "It gave me the wiggins."

"You go get a broom and clean that up, before

you even think about showing up in my kitchen for an after-school snack," Aunt Trudy told me. "I expect more out of you, Frank. You're usually so tidy and respectful of other people's things." She turned around and marched out the door.

"Do you think the snack thing applies to me, too?" Joe asked.

"Absolutely," I told him. I shook my head. "I bet no one in Justin's entourage has an Aunt Trudy."

Joe laughed. "Justin doesn't, that's for sure. He'd never get away with even a quarter of what he does if he had an Aunt T."

"Okay, now that I've established my hotel-trashing potential, let's figure out how we're going to get ourselves into Justin's entourage in the first place," I told Joe.

"Not a problem. Justin's new in town. He'll need a couple of guys to show him the happenin' Bayport spots and introduce him to the hot Bayport chiquitas."

"And those guys will bring us along?"

"I *am* those guys," Joe bragged. "All you have to do is stand next to me, and we'll be so in. As long as you don't talk much."

"There he is—Justin Carraway. Told you it would be easy finding a movie star in Bayport," Joe said.

He rubbed his hands together. "Time to work my mojo."

Justin stood about half a block away, talking to a thin girl with blond hair. "You're telling me that this famous mojo of yours can work from this distance?" I asked.

"It's a powerful thing," Joe answered. "But I'll probably have to get a tiny bit closer," he admitted after a beat.

"I really think this is a situation that cries out for a plan B," I said.

Justin kissed the blond girl. Then he turned and started walking toward us.

"Plan A is going to work just fine," Joe retorted.

Then the sound of a gunshot rang out.

And Justin Carraway went down.

Good Death

"**M**an, he does good death," I said. Justin's body had bucked and twitched just the way it should have after getting shot.

"Like that killed him," said Frank. "Didn't he get shot about twelve more times in *One Phone Call*—and then get up and fly a helicopter?"

"And?"

Frank shook his head. "What's this new movie about, anyway?"

I laughed. "You're not going to believe it. It's called *Undercover*. Justin plays a guy who is part of a secret organization that uses teenagers to solve crimes."

"Totally unbelievable, right?" a girl behind us commented.

"Totally," Frank agreed.

Justin moved a little closer to the crowd that had gathered to watch the filming, and cheering started up everywhere. Wait. I listened harder. Not everyone was cheering. There were a decent number of boos mixed in, and I heard a guy yell, "Somebody should shoot you for real, Carraway!"

"Did you hear that?" I asked Frank.

"Yeah," he told me.

I turned toward the voice, scanning the faces in that part of the crowd. I noticed that several people over in that area were holding signs. I pushed ahead a little and leaned forward so I could read them.

CLEAN UP YOUR ACT, CARRAWAY a couple of them read. MORE ACTING, LESS DRAMA! was printed in huge letters on another one. And three people held up a banner that just said CLEEN TEENS.

"What's with them, you think?" I said.

Frank had spotted the group of sign holders too. "You've never heard of Cleen Teens?" he asked.

"I don't think so," I told him.

Frank rolled his eyes. "You know the human brain has a finite capacity, don't you? Maybe you should try to forget a few of your celebrity factoids and clear up some space in there."

"Knowledge of celebrity culture has been essential

to the successful completion of many of our missions," I said, trying to sound as much as possible like my math teacher explaining an equation (otherwise known as my impression of Frank).

"I guess that's why we make a good team," Frank told me, back to sounding like a regular human. "Together we know everything that's important enough to know."

"So, Cleen Teens," I prompted.

"I want to go again, right away!" a woman working a jeans-sneaks-cowboy-hat combo called out before he could answer. I figured she had to be the director, because a bunch of crew people started rushing around. One dusted Justin's face with powder. One brushed Emily Slater's hair so it fell just the way it had at the beginning of the scene. One reloaded the gun that had been used to "shoot" Justin with blanks.

"Cleen Teens is an organization dedicated to making teenagers better citizens. It started in Delaware, but now it's a nationwide movement. Everyone—all the volunteers, the president, everybody—is eighteen or under."

I checked out the group of sign holders again. Yep, not an adult in the bunch. "So what's their problem with Justin?"

"Uh, do you think good citizens trash hotel

rooms and pretend to start fires in restaurants?" Frank asked.

"But he's just one guy. Don't they have more important things to do than stand around waving signs at him?"

"He gets thousands of fan letters a week," Frank reminded me. "He's not one guy. He's insanely famous, especially with kids his own age. That makes him a role model. I'm betting that's why the Cleen Teens are after him."

All the Cleen Teeners were behind blue police barriers. "Looks like the Bayport security has them pretty well contained," I said.

"Not just them," Frank commented. Besides the protesters, there was a whole mess of fans and a bunch of people who had to be paparazzi. Or camera salesmen. And there was plenty of security to keep all of us off the section of street where the filming was happening.

"Justin, can I get an autograph?" a girl near the front of the crowd screamed, jumping up and down with a pen in her hand.

"Sign my *Weirdness* poster!" a guy who was dressed like Justin in *Weirdness* yelled out.

"I've been waiting here since five a.m. Sign my shirt! Please!" begged a different girl.

Justin waved but didn't move any closer. "Sorry,

we're about to start up again!" he called back. "And they're still making me beautiful." He grinned, then turned his back to the crowd.

"We're definitely not going to get close enough to him to do—whatever it is you were planning to do," said Frank. "Maybe we should stake out his hotel."

"Then *we'll* look like stalkers," I answered. "Not the impression we're trying to make. There's got to be another way."

"Maybe we just got lucky," Frank said. "Isn't that the guy Justin pulled that prank on?"

I followed his gaze. "Yeah, that's him. Rick something."

"Rick Ortiz," Frank supplied.

I raised my eyebrows. "How come *you* know that? All pop culture is supposed to be stored in my half of the Team Hardy brain."

"It was part of our briefing," said Frank.

See, I was right about him and the prep. I don't mind keeping things loose, thinking on my feet. Frank likes to have a plan B, a plan C, and a plan D. He doesn't like surprises.

"Let's go talk to him." I figured Rick was heading toward the Java Joint, down at the other end of Main. I saw this reality show where people competed to win a production assistant job on a movie.

One of their tasks was remembering a coffee order for ten. And the order was really complicated. Half caf. No foam. Double foam. Only one girl got it completely right.

"What's the plan?" Frank asked.

What'd I tell you?

 FRANK

Okay, I have to step in. Plans are encouraged by ATAC. Plans are—

 JOE

You wouldn't let me talk during your part. So you don't get to talk during mine. And besides, a chunk of our ATAC training was on improvisation.

"We're winging it," I told my brother as we started after Rick. When we passed the Madison Hotel, I headed inside.

"Quick detour," I said. I walked straight over to the rack with all the brochures on local attractions. You know what I mean. They have them in every hotel everywhere. I grabbed a handful, plus a two-for-one pizza coupon. "Take some." I shoved half the brochures into Frank's hands.

"I think I see where you're going with this," said Frank. "Good plan."

"Good improvisation," I corrected. We hurried

out of the hotel lobby and on down the street. Rick disappeared into the Java Joint, just the way I thought he would. Frank and I followed him inside.

We waited until he'd put in his coffee order. A big, complicated order—I guess reality TV is actually pretty real sometimes. Then, while he was waiting for it to get filled, we made our move.

"You're Rick Ortiz, right?" I asked. "I'm Joe. That's my brother, Frank. We were wondering if you could help us out with something."

Rick fingered the mic of his wireless headset. "Guys, I'm working right now. If you want an autograph from Justin, the best way to do it is to write to him care of his production company, Just Justin. It might take a while, but you'll get one. You'll get it faster if you send in a stamped return envelope."

Rick gave out the information in a fast monotone. Sounded like he'd done it a thousand times before.

"No, that's not the deal," Frank told him. "We go to Bayport High—"

"And we were elected to welcome Justin to our town. Everyone wanted to do it, but the principal said two max," I added, holding up my brochures. "There's a coupon for a free pizza, too. Not that he needs it."

Rick laughed. "The way he eats pizza, he might be broke before the end of the year. The makeup people are always nagging him to stay away from the greasy stuff so his skin will stay clear. But Justin doesn't give a rat's long pink tail. He says it's their job to make sure any zits get covered."

He jammed his fingers in the pockets of his cargo shorts. "I can't believe I said that. You guys aren't undercover for *Star Gazer* or anything, are you?"

"No worries," Frank said. "I don't even watch that show."

The guy behind the counter started putting Rick's coffee order in cardboard trays. I grabbed one. Frank got the next one.

"Thanks," said Rick. "If you ever want to be a PA, start working on growing at least one extra hand."

"Do you think you could get us a minute with Justin? To do the welcome thing?" I asked.

"No way," Rick answered. "Uh, Justin is one of those actors who likes to stay in character until we're done for the day. Talking to fans brings him out of it," he explained. "But one of these coffees is for Sydney, Justin's publicist. She might be able to set up something later. Sounds like a good photo op."

"Cool," Frank said.

Rick crossed the street and turned down a side street a couple of blocks from where the movie was being filmed.

"Whoa," I said when I saw the row of silver trailers. One of them was three times as long as all the others. Rick stopped in front of it and knocked on the door. It was opened by Justin.

No. Not Justin. Different clothes. No makeup. But same haircut, same dent in the chin, same everything else. Ryan. The twin who "grew out of his talent," according to Sanders Smith of *Star Gazer.*

Rick reached for a cup on my tray, but Ryan held up a hand to stop him. "Justin decided he wanted one after all. He said pretending to like Emily—forget about love her—for one more minute is going to take major caffeine."

"I guess I'd better get over there fast then," Rick said. "Any chance you could take these guys over to Sydney? They're from the local high school. Want to welcome Justin. You know the drill."

Ryan nodded. "I'm sure Sydney will at least want to set up a photo. Come on. She's over in the wardrobe trailer," he told me and Frank.

"Any chance you could give this to her?" Rick held out a coffee. "It'll get cold if I don't get it to Justin first."

"Yeah, yeah. I know." Ryan took the cup. I wondered how it felt to be him. He used to be a star too. Well, at least he played half of a character that everybody loved. Now he was running errands behind the scenes on his brother's movie.

A sick thought entered my head. Could Ryan

SUSPECT PROFILE

Name: Ryan Carraway

Hometown: Chowchilla, California

Physical description: Age 17, 5'11", 150 lbs., collar-length blond hair, brown eyes, cleft chin.

Occupation: Employee of Just Justin, his brother's production company

Background: Shared a role on _Five Times Five_ with Justin, then stopped acting.

Suspicious behavior: Ended up as Justin's errand boy.

Suspected of: Being Justin's stalker.

Possible motive: Jealousy.

have written one of the threatening letters to Justin?

Did Frank and I need to protect Justin from his own brother?

It Would be Better If You Died Now

"Let's get you guys—and the coffee—over to Syd," Ryan said. He led the way down to a smaller trailer and gave a double knock on the door.

A woman in a colorful dress answered. She had on three belts and a pair of mesh gloves. "My mocha latte!" she exclaimed. "You're an angel, Ryan. Could you do me one other favor? Justin didn't think the jeans he's wearing in the elevator scene fit right. Put them on for Amanda and let her take a look, okay?"

Ryan nodded. He gave Sydney the rundown on me and Joe, then disappeared inside the trailer.

"I'm liking the looks of you two," Sydney told us.

"Very middle America, very boy-next-door. Movie boy-next-door, I mean. You're both supercute."

I felt my face get hot. Joe just grinned. "We're glad New Haven banned Justin," he said. Sydney's lips tightened, and Joe rushed on. "Because now the movie is shooting in Bayport. It's a great place. Frank and I would be happy to show Justin around, if he has any free time."

Sydney tapped her chin with one finger. "I was thinking a quick pic of you greeting Justin. But now I'm falling in love with the idea of him seeing the town with you. It's just what he needs."

"Everyone thinks making a movie would be all fun, but I guess the guy could use some R & R," Joe said.

"You're sweet," Sydney told him. "I was thinking more that Justin's image could use a little polish, and I think the combo of you two and this town could do it. Ryan will go too, of course. And Justin will want Rick along."

"How about Emily Slater?" Joe asked. "We don't want her to feel left out."

I wasn't positive who Emily Slater was, but I was betting she was the blond girl in the scene Joe and I had watched being filmed. I was pretty sure I'd seen a little trail of drool coming out of his mouth when he looked at her.

"Hmmm. Interesting idea," Sydney said. "But no. I think it should be a boys-on-the-town thing." She opened the trailer door and leaned in. "Ryan, the cute local boys are going to take you and Justin out tonight. Organize it, all right?"

Ryan stepped out of the trailer wearing new jeans. "Let me look," Sydney told him. "Turn around." Ryan obediently did a slow turn. "I don't know what Justin was talking about. They look fab." She frowned. "Amanda, you're right. The jeans are perfect. But we have to do something to them for Justin. Maybe different belt loops . . . Anything."

A loud sigh came from inside the trailer. "Fine. Just as long as you know and I know that it's completely unnecessary."

"Thanks, dolly," Sydney answered. "I've got to return a call to the local paper." She pulled out the tiniest cell phone I'd ever seen. "Ryan, take the boys over to the set. I want the paparazzi to see them welcoming Justin to town. You know the flashbulbs will start going off, and that's what we need. Remind your brother to smile."

"Elijah Gorman is out there," Ryan told Sydney.

Sydney's lips tightened again, then she forced a smile. "Just do your best." She flipped open her cell, and Ryan gestured for me and Joe to follow him.

"Who's Elijah Gorman?" I asked.

"One of the paparazzi," Ryan answered. "He's insane. He won't leave Justin alone. He actually got a shot of him in the restroom once. Justin hates the guy."

"I wouldn't be feeling the love for someone like that either," Joe commented.

"To be fair, Justin had smashed one of Elijah's cameras the day before. So Elijah wasn't exactly feeling the Justin love either. Actually, they both completely hate each other now."

"Why doesn't Elijah go after another celebrity then?" I asked.

"Pictures of Justin get top dollar. You might have noticed he's kind of popular," Ryan answered as we walked back toward the part of Main where the filming was taking place. I thought I heard a little bitterness in his voice, even though he had a smile on his face.

"Yeah, we noticed," Joe put in, jerking his chin toward the mob surrounding the shoot.

Ryan slowed down a little. "Listen, I want to ask you guys a favor. About tonight."

"What's up?" I said.

"Justin had to get insured to do this movie. I'm talking big-money insured. I don't know if you guys read the tabloids or watch shows like *Star Gazer*—"

"My brother does," I told him.

"So you know that Justin's had some . . . problems getting to the set on time. Or at all," Ryan said. "It's not that he doesn't care about the movies he's working on. It's just that he cares about having fun a little more. And when you're out all night having fun, it's kind of hard to get to work."

Joe nodded. "So you don't want Justin to have an excessive amount of fun when all of us hang out tonight."

"Exactly. If the insurance company has to pay up because Justin's behavior makes the movie run over, it's going to really hurt his career," Ryan explained.

"But like you said, he's so popular. Wouldn't everyone still want him to be in their movies?" I asked.

"They'd want him, but if he messes things up, Justin would definitely need insurance again, even more insurance than he does for this movie. The movie company has to pay for the insurance. It could make hiring him way too expensive, even for a big-budget movie," Ryan explained.

"Well, Bayport is a rockin' town," Joe said. "But I think we can manage to show your brother the sights and still get him home at a decent hour."

"All I'm asking is that you try," Ryan answered. "I know no one can actually control Justin. And even if he does manage to be responsible for once, I'm afraid the insurance company might still have to pay."

"How come?" I asked.

"Forget it. It's no big," Ryan answered.

"Sounds kinda big," Joe said. "If it's something that could stop Justin from making movies."

Ryan stopped walking. "I just meant it's probably not something that would ever happen. . . ." He looked up. "Sorry, I'm a little distracted. There's a lot going on right now."

"Everything okay?" I asked, jumping at the opportunity.

"Yeah, yeah, everything's fine. It's just . . . Justin got another stalker letter today. And it came right to the hotel. Somebody dropped it off at the front desk," he told us.

"Wait. Back up. Stalker letter?" I said.

"Yeah. All celebs get them. Creepy letters from obsessed fans. Some are even threatening. The one left at the hotel was," said Ryan.

"Do you have it on you?" Joe asked.

Ryan raised his eyebrows.

"It's just that I'm always hearing about those crazy fan letters. *Star Gazer* is always reporting on them," Joe explained.

I snorted. "Reporting, yeah," I couldn't stop myself from adding.

"Anyway, the show never gives details on what

the letters say. I'm curious about what's actually in them," Joe continued.

"I guess it wouldn't matter if I show it to you," said Ryan. He pulled a plain white envelope out of his pocket and handed it to Joe.

Joe opened the envelope carefully and then held the letter up so I could see it too. The little hairs on the back of my neck stood up as I began to read:

"You have so much, Justin. So much of everything. So much talent, so much money, so many fans. But you don't have the most important thing—self-respect. I know you don't respect yourself. I can see it. Every day you throw part of your life into the trash. Do you ever think about how much other people want your life? How much they wish they were you?

"Sometimes I think it would be better if you just died now. Then maybe someone who deserved it would get some of what you have. Some of your opportunities. The right person with your money and influence could change the world. I guess you change it too—but you make it worse. The more I think about it, the more convinced I am that the world would be a better place if you just died. Now."

"That is freakier than I thought it would be," Joe said. "I guess when I think of stalkers, I kind of think of girls who are way too in love with you and are going to follow you around everywhere until you say you'll go to the prom with them."

"Justin definitely has some of that kind of stalker," Ryan answered. "But he has people who want to hurt him too. Like whoever wrote this letter." He took it back from Joe. "Probably the writer will never do more than just write another twisted letter. But what if they want Justin dead so badly that they would actually try to make it happen? Sometimes I think it's possible that somebody is going to try to murder my brother."

JOE

7

All About the Fun

Ryan told the security guards that we were with him—and just like that, we were on the other side of the barriers. Pretty cool, huh?

"Hey, bro!" Justin called out. "Everyone has been told I want a shot of chocolate in my coffee, right?"

"Slick's told them. Sydney's told them. I've told them," Ryan answered, leading us over to Justin.

"So why did I just get coffee with no chocolaty goodness at all?" Justin asked.

"Because it was *my* coffee. You didn't ask for any, then you decided you wanted some, so you got mine. And you know I'm allergic to chocolate," Ryan explained.

"You're allergic to everything. You should see his

43

allergy pills. He has a whole pill box full of them. He's like a little old lady," said Justin, talking to me and Frank like we were already buds. Then he wrapped one arm around his brother's shoulders. "You didn't have to give up your drink. Rick could have made another run. That's his job."

"He was busy," Ryan answered.

"Too busy to get me coffee? Dude, it was essential. I could not get myself to act like I wanted to be near Emily without some chemical stimulation. So without the coffee, no scene. Rick has to get his priorities in line." Justin's voice got louder, and his eyes started to bug out. He poured the cup of coffee he held out onto the ground. "No coffee with chocolate, and the movie shuts down, and he— along with everybody else—loses his job." He was screaming now.

Then suddenly he laughed. He had one of those laughs that make you want to laugh too. And I did. So did Frank. And Ryan.

"I had you guys going for a minute. Admit it," Justin said to me and Frank.

"I admit it," said Frank.

"You got me, too," I agreed.

"I figured you deserved a little show," Justin told us. "You couldn't say you'd met Justin Carraway and he was totally normal and well behaved, am I right? That would be no fun."

"My brother's all about the fun," Ryan said.

"*My* brother's all about the work," Justin countered. "So did you two win backstage passes on the radio or something?" he asked me and Frank.

"They're the welcoming committee from Bayport High," Ryan explained. "Syd wants us all to hang tonight. They're going to show us the town."

Justin took the brochures I still held in my hand. "Folk art museum—boring. Scenic bus tour—boring. Colonial times re-enactment—boring. Pizza coupon—I'll be keeping this. Firehouse museum—boring." Justin handed the brochures back. "What I'm thinking for tonight is a private party at the hotel. Maybe a little poker. You play?"

"I have more toothpicks than anyone else combined," I boasted. "That's what we play for—toothpicks," I explained.

"I usually play for cash," said Justin. "But I'm kind of out of your league in that department, so toothpicks it is. So can you round up a few players?"

"Sure," I said.

"Invite some girls, too. I feel like meeting some new people," Justin added.

"Finding girls willing to hang with you?" I asked. "It'll be tough, but we can call in some favors."

Justin laughed. So did Frank and I. But this time, Ryan didn't even smile.

"What?" Justin asked.

"Like you don't know," Ryan answered. He turned to me and Frank. "Justin uses girls up like Kleenex. Goes out with them once or twice, then throws them in the garbage."

I flashed on part of the letter Ryan had shown us. *Every day you throw part of your life into the trash.* It was similar to what Ryan had just said.

"Come on, I'm seventeen. I'm not supposed to be getting married anytime soon," Justin retorted. "And, in case you've forgotten, Ryan, you're seventeen too. Stop worrying about everything all the time. Worry when you're old."

"Whatever. I just think you're trashing things—people—that are worth keeping. Very worth keeping," Ryan said.

"Like Emily," stated Justin. And it was like Frank and I had disappeared. The two brothers faced off, ignoring everything else.

"Yeah, like Emily," Ryan agreed.

"The only reason you care is because you have a crush on her," Justin snapped. "You should be glad I dumped her. Now you can have your shot."

"Right. She can't stand to look at you because you hurt her so bad," Ryan shot back. "She's not going to be able to get past it. When she looks at me, she still sees you. Which means she can't stand to look at me, either."

"Sorry I messed that up for you, bro," said Justin. "At least you can still drive that car I bought you, and swim in the pool at the house I paid for, and travel anywhere you want to go on my dime."

"I still have *Five Times Five* money," Ryan protested.

"Only because I pay for everything," Justin told him. "I pay your credit card bills, bro. I bought you your Maserati. Wherever we go, I pick up the tab."

Ryan's eyes narrowed.

"Truth hurts, doesn't it?" Justin taunted.

Ryan's hands tightened into fists.

"You going to hit me now?" Justin demanded.

Cleen vs. Clean

I shot a glance at Joe. Should we be stepping in?

"I know you won't do it," Justin taunted.

Ryan's jaw clenched. I didn't know if he'd hit his brother or not. But I was pretty sure he wanted to.

Rick hurried over and joined us. "Five minutes, Justin," he said. "And so you know, some of the paps have their telephoto lenses geared up. I don't think that was the kind of photo op Sydney was hoping for."

Ryan immediately took a step away from Justin. "Syd wants you to let these guys do an official welcome, let the paparazzi get some pictures no one has to be ashamed of—for once," he said, his voice emotionless.

"I'm not ashamed of anything I do," Justin told him. He turned to Rick. "Go get a couple of the paps. Not Elijah. The hot girl from *Know This*. Whoever else you want."

"Excluding him is only going to make him go after you harder," Ryan said. "Do you want to have another picture of yourself in the bathroom all over the net?"

"What do I care? All my friends thought it was hilarious," said Justin. "I think I'll start eating chili every meal so I'll be prepared to let some stink bombs fly if Elijah does try it."

Ryan rubbed his eyes, like he was suddenly incredibly tired.

"Come on, Ryan. I'm just using one of your old tricks," Justin said. "You used to save up your farts like ammunition. Remember how you used to turn the air in the bathroom foul before our on-set tutor went in there?"

"Bean burritos with garlic. Plus lots of soda for extra gas," Ryan answered. And he actually smiled.

I guess these two couldn't stay mad at each other. Joe and I are like that. I can be wishing I was an only child, then Joe will say something that cracks me up. And it's pretty much impossible to stay mad when you're laughing.

"The boy was a genius," Justin told me and Joe.

"Still is. He keeps things running smooth for me."

Rick returned with four photographers, and suddenly Sydney materialized. "These boys are Frank and Joe Hardy. They go to Bayport High, and they're here to welcome Justin to town. In fact, they are going to take him out to see the sights tonight."

I shook hands with Justin. Then Joe did.

Flash. Flash. Flash.

"Where are you going to take him?" one of the paparazzi called out.

"Folk art museum," Joe deadpanned.

"Followed by a bus tour of scenic downtown," Justin added, his smile getting wider. "Now I've got to get back on the set. See you later, dudes. Bring plenty of toothpicks. You're going to need them."

The photographers followed Justin as he headed over to the section of Main where the shoot was taking place. Sydney hurried after them.

"I've got some stuff to take care of," Ryan said. "You guys can watch the filming from over there if you want." He pointed to a couple of empty canvas chairs behind a monitor. The director stood nearby.

"Excellent," said Joe.

"Come on over to the hotel about eight," Ryan added. "Bring whoever you want. But keep the number manageable, okay? If the party gets too out of control, Justin could end up banned from a new place."

"Let's talk suspects," I said after Ryan was out of earshot.

"I think one might have just been standing here talking to us," Joe noted.

"Me too," I agreed. "Did you notice that he talked about Justin throwing girls into the garbage? Just like the letter Ryan showed us." I frowned. "But then almost right after Ryan seemed like he was about to punch Justin, Justin got him laughing."

"Yeah. Maybe Ryan shouldn't be at the top of our suspect list. But we've got other contenders." Joe looked over at the little cluster of Cleen Teeners. Most of them had started to boo now that Justin was getting ready to perform again.

"Let's see what we can find out. Two middle-America boy-next-door types should be welcome over there," I said.

"But . . . director's chairs." Joe looked longingly at the empty chairs right next to the director.

"But . . . mission," I said.

"Right." Joe and I left the secure area and dove back into the crowd. We worked our way to Cleen Teens central. "Hey, that's Caro Whittier." Joe pointed to a girl in the middle of the CT group.

Caro's this girl who goes to Bayport High. I've

never really talked to her. But I figured my brother had. He doesn't have the blushing issue. "Do you know her?"

"We were lab partners for a semester last year," Joe told me. "She was always whipping out this little bottle of hand sanitizer. So I knew she was clean. But I didn't know she was Cleen."

"Let's use her as our in," I suggested.

Joe nodded and changed course slightly so that we were heading directly for Caro. "Hi," Joe said when we reached her. "You cut class too, huh?" We'd had to skip school today to be here when the shoot started. I have to admit, I'd gotten pretty good at forging those "please excuse" notes with one of our parents' signatures.

"I've never cut," Caro replied. "My parents gave me permission to miss school today. They are really behind the Cleen Teen cause."

"Maybe I should join. I wouldn't mind having parental permission to cut," Joe teased.

Caro didn't seem to think he was funny. "Cleen Teens is a serious organization. We've actually gotten some legislation changes to give harsher sentences to underage drunk drivers. And we've organized Promise to Stay Cleen pledges all over the country. I'm in charge of heading it up in Bayport during the fall."

"That's, uh, great," Joe said. "Put me down."

Now Caro smiled. "Really? You'd be interested in helping out?"

"Definitely. Frank too," Joe told her.

"Awesome. You guys have to meet William Bost. He's the president of the national group. I know he'll want to talk to you. Be back in a sec." Caro squeezed between two other protesters and vanished into the mob.

"You know we're going to have to work on the pledge thing now," said Joe. "She will hunt me down if we don't."

"It doesn't seem like a bad group. I'm for a lot of what they're for," I answered.

"Unless they threaten people to get what they're for," Joe said.

"Unless that," I agreed.

Caro returned with a stocky, dark-haired guy. I wondered if he was the one who had yelled, "Someone should shoot you for real, Carraway!"

"This is William," Caro said proudly.

"Good to meet you," William greeted us. He stuck out his hand. I shook, and felt something sticky on my fingers. I looked down at them. "Oops. Sorry," said William. "I was just eating a Goo Goo Cluster."

"A what?"

"It's this candy they have in the South," Caro said. "William never leaves home without a box."

"They're good, but really, well, gooey," William said, licking some chocolate off his palm.

Caro wrinkled her nose, then pulled a small bottle of hand sanitizer out of her purse. She offered me a squirt, which I took, then held the bottle out to William. "I'm good," he said, giving his fingers a last lick. Unlike Caro, he clearly was just about the Cleen, not the clean.

"Caro told us your group has gotten some changes in drunk-driving legislation," I told him. "That's really impressive. You're really making a difference. Who knows how many lives you'll have saved?"

I've found flattery a useful tool when I'm trying to get info. But I meant it too. I did think working against drunk driving was vital.

"But I don't get what you're doing here," I went on. I'd already given Joe my theory on why the group was so focused on Justin, but I wanted to hear what William would say.

William pulled another Goo Goo Cluster out of his shirt pocket and began to unwrap the candy as he talked. "If Justin Carraway joined our group, it would be the equivalent of millions of dollars of advertising. Reporters would write about our group every time Justin mentioned it—and forget about what would happen if he attended some events."

"So you want him as a spokesman?" Joe asked.

"That would be awesome," William said. "But before Justin could ever become a spokesman for Cleen Teens, he'd have to get his act together. Right now, that's what we're focused on. Even if Justin never becomes interested in the group, he could influence so many teenagers to become better citizens and people just by changing his own behavior."

"Right now he's more of a poster boy for what not to do," Caro added. She flicked the top of her hand sanitizer open and closed, staring at William's fingers. They were already chocolate-coated again.

William looked over to where Justin and Emily were getting some last-minute instructions from the director. "If he could only turn himself around, he could change the whole world with his influence."

I shot a fast glance at Joe, and I knew he'd realized the same thing I had. William had almost quoted a part of the stalker letter Ryan had showed us.

SUSPECT PROFILE

Name: William Bost

Hometown: Huntersville, North Carolina

"The way he is right now, he's influencing people to be the opposite of Cleen Teens," Caro added. "Like Emily Slater. She used to be the perfect role model for teens. She always talked about animal rights and going green in her interviews. And you never saw her behaving badly on one of those TV shows that are all about celebrities. There were never any negative magazine articles. But now—"

"Now she's turning into a girl version of Justin," William finished for her. "She isn't any kind of role model anymore. I just saw a news story about her throwing a glass of water at a waiter. He had to go to the hospital to be treated for a possible concussion."

"And in an interview I read last week, she was raving about a new liquid diet she's on. Eating disorders are a big problem with lots of teenage girls. And it's like Emily has become a spokesperson for anorexia," Caro said. "I find her—"

"We need quiet. Quiet please," a man in a Hawaiian shirt called to the crowd.

It took a few moments, but the crowd hushed. Justin lay down in the street, a puddle of fake blood running off his shirt and down to the asphalt.

Hawaiian Shirt stepped in front of him. "Scene forty-seven, take one," he announced, slapping one of those movie clapboards together. I'd never seen anybody do that in real life.

Emily let out a high shriek and raced toward Justin. She dropped down on her knees next to him and cradled him against her body, murmuring into his ear.

Then she sprang to her feet, letting Justin fall back. "I can't believe you!" she shouted.

Justin jumped up. "What? You're saying it's not true?" he yelled back.

Flash, flash, flash. Flash, flash. The paparazzi were going nuts, firing off shots of Justin and Emily.

"Cut!" the director called. "What just happened?" she demanded.

"She was whispering stupid stuff in my ear, trying to make me break character," Justin answered.

"Only because he—," Emily began.

"I didn't do anything," Justin interrupted.

"You're actually saying that. When you know you hurt me so bad," Emily exclaimed.

"I told you I didn't want to hurt you," Justin told her.

"Well, you did. And you knew it while you were doing it," Emily cried.

"Over here, Emily!" Elijah called. She turned her head. Elijah snapped picture after picture, along with the rest of the photographers.

"How can we fix this?" asked the director. "What needs to happen so you two can work together for more than one minute at a time?"

"Kill him," Emily answered. "I could definitely do the scene if I was really holding his dead body."

And the suspects kept on comin'.

SUSPECT PROFILE

Name: Emily Slater

Hometown: Pawtucket, Rhode Island

Physical description: Age 17, 5'6", 115 lbs., long blond hair, green eyes.

Occupation: Actor

Background: Discovered while performing in a high school play by a friend's director father. Played the best friend in a short-lived TV show. _Undercover_ is her first film.

Suspicious behavior: Announced that she'd like someone to kill Justin.

Suspected of: Being Justin's stalker.

Possible motive: Heartbroken after Justin broke up with her.

The Dillweed

"That's enough!" the director yelled at Justin and Emily. "I'm starting to feel like a kindergarten teacher. I'm trying to make a movie here."

"Keep her away from me," Justin yelled back. "When we don't have a scene together, I want her to be kept one hundred feet away. Ryan, call Slick. Tell him to get my lawyer to slap a restraining order on her. You heard her say she wants me dead!"

"I want a restraining order too!" Emily screamed.

Elijah ducked under one of the barriers and crept closer, circling around Emily and Ryan to get a photo from a different angle.

"Ryan, tell Slick that my restraining order has to include my trailer." He whipped his head back toward Emily. "You're the one stealing from me, aren't you? You're a complete stalker."

"Slap him, Emily!" Elijah coached. "He deserves to be slapped for that."

Justin jerked around toward the photographer. With two long strides, he was on Elijah. He grabbed Elijah's camera, hurled it to the ground, then stomped on it. "I want a restraining order on you, too!" Justin bellowed.

"I said enough!" the director snapped. "Back to your starting places, both of you. Somebody fix the blood. The pool on the street is all smeared now, thanks to the foot stomping and leg kicking from the children." She sucked in a deep breath. "And you!" She pointed at Elijah. "You're out of here." She signaled to one of the security guards.

"This is public property—," Elijah began.

"And we have a permit to use it," the director answered as a security guard took Elijah by the arm. "Didn't you two hear me?" she asked, her attention on Justin and Emily again.

Sydney did her reappearing act. One minute she was nowhere, the next right in the middle of things.

"He heard you, he heard you," she said, patting the director's arm with one gloved hand, while waving Justin back into place with the other.

Justin opened his mouth, like he wanted to say more. But he lay back down on the street without another word. Emily stalked over to her initial position in silence. Nobody looked happy. Not Justin, not Emily, not the director, not Sydney. Definitely not the Cleen Teens.

Caro clucked her tongue. "Emily never would have thrown a tantrum like that before she met Justin."

Guess Frank and I were going to have to find a chance to talk to Emily. She had just announced that she'd rather work with Justin's dead body than the live version. You know, sometimes being an ATAC agent is really hard. Having to go up and talk to beautiful movie stars and all.

Actually, for Frank that probably is the hard part of the job. There are times I'm very glad I'm not my brother.

 FRANK

Okay, okay, I know it's your turn, but can you stick to the story if it's your turn to tell it?

 JOE

You've got one thing right, Frank—it's still *my* turn. Anyway, as I was saying . . . Hawaiian Shirt slammed the clapboard down, announcing the second take of Scene 47. Again, Emily ran toward Justin and dropped down next to him. She cradled him close . . . then started to laugh.

"Cut!" the director yelled.

"I'm sorry, I'm sorry," Emily exclaimed, scrambling to her feet. "I just . . . I don't know. Seeing him lying in the blood and everything." She giggled.

"That's it for today," said the director, her face flushed with anger. "Shut it down!" she called to the crew.

"Guess we should head home too," I said to Frank as the crowd began to break up. "We've got phone calls to make and toothpicks to acquire."

"Who do you think we should ask?" Frank said. "After what we just saw, I'm not sure how much fun this party is going to be for anyone. I doubt Justin's going to be in a happy mood."

"Even if it's not *fun* fun, everyone we know is going to want to be there," I reasoned.

"So who?" Frank asked.

I thought about it as we walked. We hadn't bothered to take our motorcycles. We had figured there'd be no place to park even a cycle anywhere near the shoot, and we'd been right. "Chet, for sure," I said, naming the guy who'd been our best friend since forever.

We managed to come up with four more people—two more guys and two girls—by the time we reached our front walk.

"Hey, we forgot about Dad," I said to Frank.

"What?"

"You know Dad will want to be there," I told him. "He'll want to make sure we're safe."

Frank stared at me for a long moment. Then he cracked up. So did I. We'd been working really hard to train our father to treat us like any other ATAC agents. Meaning hands off. Letting us use all the hours and hours of prep ATAC had given us to complete our mission in the way we thought was best.

We were still laughing when we walked in the front door.

"Something funny?" Dad asked as we passed through the living room. The question made us laugh harder.

"Don't get so caught up in the fun part of—" He lowered his voice. "Your mission. Hanging out with movie stars and all that. You have to stay alert. Always. You two could be all that stops Justin Carraway from getting attacked or worse."

That killed the laughter. Was Dad ever going to get that we were really good agents? Not agents-in-training? That we had already stopped people from getting attacked—or worse—without him to remind us?

"We're always on alert when we're working, Dad," Frank said. I knew he'd been thinking pretty much what I had.

Dad sighed. "I know that. I trust you. I trust all the agents. But I'm always going to worry about you more. It's not only Justin who could get hurt. You're always in danger too. Every mission. There are times I wish I'd never brought you into ATAC. Except you are exactly the kind of kids— agents—I had in mind when I founded the organization."

Wow. I never thought I'd hear Dad say that.

"Thanks," said Frank.

"Thanks," I echoed. But I couldn't help adding, "Now excuse us, we have to go get ready to par-tay!"

I couldn't believe what I saw when Frank and I walked into the lobby of the Fairmont Hotel, where Justin was staying.

"What—" Frank didn't seem able to complete his thought.

"What is Chet wearing?" I finished for him.

Frank nodded.

"It appears to be a T-shirt with lapels and a bow tie drawn on it to give it, unsuccessfully, the appearance of a tuxedo jacket," I said. "And a pair of purple pants made of some extremely shiny material I am unable to identify."

"Hey, guys. I decided to wait for you down here," Chet said as he hurried over to us. "I didn't want to go up to the room without you. Even though I know I'm invited and everything. I'm invited, right?"

"You are totally invited," said Frank. Even though I'd told him exactly what Chet was wearing, he was still staring at our friend like he was trying to figure it out.

"And also, I kind of wanted to keep watching her." Chet nodded toward the front desk. For the first time, I realized that Emily Slater was standing in front of it. Now you know exactly how startling Chet's outfit was. "Is she going to be at the party too?"

"Doubtful," I answered. "Extremely doubtful."

"She and Justin aren't really friends," Frank added. Understatement of the decade.

"Why don't you two go on up to the room? I'll wait down here. The other guys might want someone to go in with too," I suggested.

Frank flicked his eyes toward Emily, then back to me. "Good idea," he said, and I knew he'd figured out that I wanted to use the opportunity to talk to one of our suspects. I think he was relieved he didn't have to do it himself.

I waited until Chet and Frank were on the elevator, then walked over to Emily. "Hi, I'm Joe Hardy," I told her. "I'm part of the Bayport High committee to welcome you and the rest of the movie group to Bayport."

"I think I saw you talking to Justin before," she answered, sounding as if she'd already decided not to like me because of that.

The clerk passed a key across the counter to Emily. "If you have any problems with your new room, don't hesitate to let us know. I'm sure we can find something you like, Miss Slater."

"I'm sure this one will be perfect," Emily answered. She started toward the elevator.

"Let me guess. The room is as far away from Justin's as possible," I said. "I saw the—" Would she be offended if I called it a fight? It was totally a fight. But maybe that would make it sound like I thought she had—

"You saw the enormous shouting match between us?" Emily supplied.

"Yeah. It seemed like he was being a dillweed," I told her.

And she smiled. Going with the enemy-of-my-enemy-is-my-friend strategy usually works. "He so was," she answered. "Like accusing me of taking stuff from his trailer. As if I would want to touch anything that belongs to him."

"Want me to kill him for you?" I joked. The elevator pinged, then the doors opened. We both stepped on.

"I shouldn't have said that. I shouldn't have gotten into it with him at all," said Emily. "It made me look so bad in front of the director and the whole crew."

"I'm pretty sure that there were two people in the fight," I commented.

"Yeah, but it's not going to hurt Justin. First of all, he charms practically everybody. I don't know how he does it. He acts like a complete jerk, then he makes a joke or gives that smile of his, and—bam! All's forgiven and forgotten."

"And second of all?" I prompted.

"Second of all, he's Justin Carraway. People are going to go see our movie because he's in it. He's the box office draw. I could be replaced by a hundred other actresses. The girl who's Lola on *Heartache*? She would kill to have my part."

Since I figured Lola wouldn't kill to have Justin's part, I didn't add her name to the suspect list. Unless she wanted to do it dressed as a guy, which would probably be good Oscar bait. . . .

The elevator pinged again and the doors opened. The ride was over way too fast. "This is my floor,"

Emily said. "Where were you going?" She looked over at the panel of buttons. None were lit, because I hadn't pressed one.

"Uh, actually, I'm going to a party in Justin's suite," I admitted. "Part of the whole welcoming thing."

"Oh." Icicles were hanging from that little word.

"Not that I want to. Who wants to hang with a dillweed? But I was kind of elected by my class," I explained.

"Want to blow it off for a while and hang with me instead?" she asked, the icicles melted. "You said you were supposed to be welcoming me, too."

"Definitely."

Emily led the way to her room and swiped her new key card through the lock. "We can raid the minibar. The movie company is paying for everything, so we can even get the macadamia nuts. Even though they cost, like, a dollar a nut at this place." She shook her head. "I must sound like a dork. Excited about free macadamia nuts. But this is the first time I've worked on location. Staying in a hotel and all that."

"My adrenaline is pumping just thinking about free macadamia nuts," I told her.

She laughed. "Confession? I've never even stayed in a hotel with a minibar before. When my mom and I drove out to L.A. so I could go to auditions last year, it was Motel Eleven all the way."

"But you have to admit, the free ice at Motel Eleven's pretty exciting," I said.

"I bet Justin doesn't even know what a Motel Eleven is. He's been rich and famous since before he learned his first word. He's had everything, always." A little anger crept into her voice. "I don't want to keep talking about him. He's not worthy of conversation." Emily grabbed a diet soda and some nuts out of the fridge. She tossed the nuts to me.

"You're letting me get first dibs?" I asked. "That could be dangerous. I could inhale this whole can with no effort."

"Go ahead. I don't think I'll have any right now," Emily said, her eyes darkening a little. I remembered what Caro said about Emily being on some kind of liquid diet.

"Come on," I urged. "Your first minibar experience and you're having a soda?"

"Justin was always—I said I wasn't talking about him anymore," she burst out. "You go ahead and inhale. I'm really not hungry right now."

"He was always what?" I wanted to know.

I got that she didn't want to talk about her ex. But I needed to hear how she felt about Justin. *She's still a suspect*, I reminded myself.

"Nothing," she said.

I waited. Usually if you wait and don't say anything, the other person will talk to fill up the silence.

"Justin was always telling me that Rhode Island thin isn't Hollywood thin, and that I had to be really careful about what I ate," Emily continued in a rush. "Maybe that's even why he broke up with me. I'm Rhode Island thin."

See? It works.

"It sounds like Jus—the dillweed," I corrected myself. "It sounds like he breaks up with girls all the time. Am I supposed to believe that every one of them didn't meet some skinniness standard of his?"

"I guess not." She unscrewed the top of her diet soda. "It's not like I didn't know about the other girlfriends. It's impossible not to know if you're alive and have a television. But I guess I stupidly believed that what the two of us had was different. Real."

Emily took a long gulp of soda. "So would you really kill him for me?" she asked, her eyes shiny with unshed tears. "Because sometimes, it's honestly the only thing I can think of that would make me feel better."

Party Crashers

"**A**ll in." I pushed my little pile of toothpicks into the center of the table.

"He's bluffing," Andrew said.

Justin studied my face. "I'm an actor, and I know when someone is acting," he said.

I tensed a little before I could stop myself. I actually *was* acting. I was acting like I had horrible cards, when my hand was great. I wanted out of the game so I could get some info out of Ryan, who was already in the losers' lounge.

"So is he acting or not?" Eli, another friend we'd invited, asked.

"Like I'm telling," Justin answered. "This is a cutthroat competition we got going here. I win, and

I'll never have to buy toothpicks again."

Chet raised. I had been counting on that. Chet always went for the I'm-worried-about-my-hand face I was working. "I fold," I said when the bidding reached me again.

"Got another loser to keep you company, Ryan," Justin yelled cheerfully.

"Want me to pop in *Skull Face Five*?" Ryan asked. "Justin always gets copies of movies before they're released."

"Cool," I said. I flopped down on the couch next to him. "Although I don't think anything is going to creep me out the way that letter you showed me today did." I looked over my shoulder at the poker players. They were all totally caught up in the game. Well, Rick and Justin were. The rest of the players—the guys and girls Joe and I had invited—were more into the thrill of sitting at a table with a star. "I mean, it really sounded like someone out there wants your brother dead."

"More than one someone, if you believe the letters he gets. We've been getting a ton of the threatening ones lately. Today's was the first one that was delivered by hand, though. That actually gives me the creeps too."

Ryan switched the *Skull Face* DVD from hand to hand. "Usually I think of the threats as just threats, you know. Basically just noise. Trash talk, whatever. But I know the person who wrote the letter I showed you is close. He—or she, I guess—walked right into this hotel. He was probably in the crowd today. Watching Justin. Maybe he's even back in the hotel tonight." Ryan tossed the DVD on the coffee table. "I keep wondering if maybe Justin has a real stalker now. Someone who is going to do a lot more than just write a letter."

He sounded genuinely concerned about his brother. *He's an actor too*, I told myself.

That reminded me of something else I wanted to talk to Ryan about. I just had to move the conversation where I needed it to go. "I'm surprised you hit the losers' lounge before I did," I began. "You're an actor too. You should be a master of the bluff."

"I haven't been an actor in a long time," Ryan answered. "Not since *Five Times Five* went off the air, and that was when I was eleven."

"You miss it?" I asked.

Now it was Ryan checking to see if anyone at the poker table was listening in. "Sometimes," he admitted.

"Why not get back into it then?"

"Justin and I played the same character on the show, because when it started we were so little that we could each work only limited hours a day. Child labor laws. But by the time it ended, we were old enough that each of us could work enough hours to play our own part."

Ryan picked up the DVD and started switching it from hand to hand again. Was the conversation making him nervous? If it was, I was on the right track.

"Our manager, Slick, he thought it would be too hard for both of us to be out there auditioning. We'd always be competing with each other. It's hard enough for one person to build up a name. Forget about two when they look exactly alike. We'd basically get parts playing twins and that's it."

"I got you," I said. "But how'd you decide who was going to be the one who kept acting? Flip a coin?"

Ryan hesitated. "What I tell reporters when they ask that, is that I just wanted to be a regular kid. That I didn't want to act anymore when the show went off the air."

"But?"

"But really, Slick made the call. He said that Justin and I were both 'really talented,' but that Justin had this 'spark' that I didn't." Ryan glanced over at his brother. "I guess he was right. Justin throws tantrums and acts like a spoiled brat a lot of the time. But people still love him. He makes them love him somehow."

I didn't know what to say. What do you say to that? People love you, too, Ryan? I'd just met the guy. I couldn't tell him that without it sounding completely fake. And truth? People did respond differently to Justin and Ryan. Part of that had to be because Justin was the star at this point. But Justin also had this way of making you feel like you were his bud when you'd barely met him. Ryan . . . didn't.

"Slick made the right call," Ryan added. He stood up. "I need to go take my allergy medicine." He hurried into the bathroom.

I felt kind of bad. I'd made him talk about stuff that he'd probably rather forget. I tried to imagine how I'd feel if ATAC suddenly decided that they could only use Joe or me as an agent, not both. And then they said they thought Joe had something I didn't that made him better, even though we were both "talented."

I love my brother. Not like I go around telling him that. And I know he loves me, too. But if ATAC chose Joe over me, it would be hard to deal with. I'd want to be happy for him, but I really don't know if I'd be able to pull it off.

I know one thing for sure, though—I wouldn't want to hurt him. I wouldn't want him dead. But I wasn't Ryan. Maybe Ryan thought that if he killed

Justin, he'd be able to become the star.

A knock on the door jerked me away from my thoughts. "Ryan, will you get that?" Justin called.

"I'll do it. He's in the bathroom," I said. I got up and opened the door. One of the last people I wanted to see stood there. Brian Conrad.

"Now the party can get started!" Brian announced. He swaggered into the suite. His sister, Belinda, followed more slowly. Her eyes went directly to Justin.

"More party people. All right!" Justin stood up. "We've got a poker game going. The movie is going to shoot in Atlantic City when we're done here, and I wanted to get some practice in."

"I'm in," Brian said.

"Take my chair. It's hot," Justin told him, then headed over to Belinda. "I have this sudden intense need to dance." He held out his hand. She took it. And I figured it was too late to mention that Brian—and Belinda—had completely crashed the party.

There was another knock on the door. More crashers?

Nope. My brother. He surveyed the scene, then slapped me on the shoulder. "Guess you don't have to worry about Belinda crushing on you anymore. I know how much you hated that."

I didn't hate it. Not exactly. I just didn't know what I wanted to do about it.

"I guess Brian heard about the party," I said. "He and Belinda just showed up."

"And clearly Justin was okay with that. At least the Belinda part," Joe pointed out. "I wonder if they even realize that they're dancing slow to a fast song?"

"Ryan's on it." He was over by the sound system, flipping through CDs. "And at least Justin's easy to keep an eye on right now," I commented. "He's safe."

"I don't know," Joe joked. "Belinda looks like she wouldn't mind kidnapping him right about now."

Before I could answer, there was yet another knock on the door. I decided to keep playing door-man. Since Joe and I were supposed to be protecting Justin, it seemed like a good idea to be the first one to see anyone coming into the room.

I opened the door. Room service.

I'd heard Ryan put in a big order, so I opened the door wider. The room service guy rolled a table inside.

I realized several things almost at once. The guy was wearing a wig. He had on sneakers—not part of the hotel uniform. And I'd seen him before.

He didn't work at the hotel! The guy leaned down and reached for something under the table. Something metallic.

A gun!

Whoa

"Joe!" Frank yelled at me. "To your left."

I whipped around and saw the room service guy pulling something shiny out from under the rolling table.

Gun!

I started toward him, shoulder low, aiming for the spot behind his knees. I could tackle him then—

Wait. That wasn't a gun in his hand. It was a camera.

He aimed it at Justin and Belinda. Flash, flash, flash.

And then I got it. It was Elijah Gorman, the photographer whose camera Justin had smashed today. He'd gotten in disguised as the room service dude.

Justin let out a howl of fury. And then he did what I'd been planning to do. He threw himself at Elijah and knocked him to the ground.

"I told you to stay away from me!" Justin shouted. He reached behind him and grabbed a lamp off one of the end tables. He raised it over his head, looking ready to bring it down on Elijah's face.

"Justin, don't!" Ryan yelled. I grabbed the cord coming out of the base of the lamp and gave it a hard yank. The motion pulled Justin back a few steps.

"What are you doing?" Justin shouted at me, giving Elijah the opportunity to scramble to his feet. He started for the door, camera hugged to his chest.

Justin snatched a crystal bowl off the coffee table and hurled it at Elijah. He missed. The bowl slammed against the door and shattered. Kayla McHugh, another friend we'd invited, screamed.

Elijah darted out of the door, and about three seconds later, Sydney rushed in. "What just happened?" she demanded. "I heard room-destroying sounds. You're supposed to be having a little party. That's all!"

"Elijah just snuck in and started taking pictures!" Justin yelled. "I told you I don't want that leech within a hundred feet of me."

"Did he get a picture of you doing that?" Sydney

pointed at the crystal shards on the floor.

"No, he was too busy running," answered Justin, sounding proud of himself.

"Justin was really brave," Belinda said.

"No, Justin was really stupid," Sydney snapped.

"I can fire you, you know," Justin told her. "You work for me."

"And I'm sure there are publicists lining up in front of the hotel to take my place," Sydney shot back. "Everybody wants to work for the boy who needs his image repaired on a daily basis. I don't have any life because of you. I wanted to have a few hours to myself. Hang in my room, read a book. But you always need damage control."

She sucked in a deep breath. "I'm going to go find Elijah and find a way—some way—to make sure your rampage doesn't go public."

"But he's the one who snuck in here!" Justin protested. "Right into my room."

"Did he throw anything at you?" Sydney countered.

Justin didn't answer.

"That's what I thought," said Sydney. She turned on her heel and strode out into the hallway.

"Whoa," I said softly.

"Yeah," Frank agreed.

Less than a minute later, Sydney was back—with

a big smile on her face. "Taken care of," she said cheerfully. "He'll sell a couple of nice party pics and keep his mouth shut about everything else."

Justin came over and gave her a hug. "Everybody should have a Sydney," he announced to the group. "She's fierce. She's smart. She's dedicated. And look how cute she is."

"Excuse us for having that little tiff in front of you," Sydney said. "Justin and I—and Ryan, too—we're like family. We yell at each other sometimes, but we love each other. Justin actually made me a Mother's Day card, back when he was on *Five Times Five*. It had a duckling made out of yellow yarn on the front. Isn't that adorable?"

"So adorable," said Belinda.

"Ryan, you have a box of *Get Desmond* DVDs that Justin autographed in your room, right?" Sydney asked.

Ryan nodded.

"Run get it. Everyone at the party should have one. And you should all feel special. It won't drop in stores for another two weeks," Sydney said.

"Cool!" Chet exclaimed.

Ryan returned to the living room of the suite with a stack of DVDs in his hands. He quickly passed them out.

"Now stop standing around. Have fun. Dance!

Eat!" Sydney began pulling covers off the dishes on the table. "Did you notice that you had no problem getting your chicken-liver-and-apple dip? I called ahead to make sure the hotel chef knew it was your favorite."

"And you got replacements for the stuff stolen out of my trailer?" asked Justin.

"New brush—natural boar bristles, oval, your initials in platinum, dark wood. New pendant—Zen symbol, stainless steel and teak, rubber cord. New dental flossers—red plastic, mint-flavored floss," she rattled off.

Justin pointed at her. "So cute!"

She pointed back at him. "So cute!" She gave the rest of us a wave as she headed for the door. "Have fun!" she called over her shoulder.

"You heard her. Let's have some fun!" Justin cranked up the music and started dancing with Belinda again. Kayla and Andrew started dancing too. Chet and our friend Maddy returned to the poker table.

Ryan popped the DVD into the player. "I've already seen this once," he told me and Joe. "It'll be cool video wallpaper with the sound off and the music on." He wandered over to the minibar and got himself a soda.

Weirdly, the gorefest on the screen started making me hungry. No, that sounds ick. I mean I got hungry even though I was watching a gorefest. I headed over to the table of food. "Which one is the chicken liver spread?" I called to Justin.

"That one." Justin pointed to a bowl of gray goop.

"I'm leavin' it all for you," I told him. It was definitely not anything I had any interest in ingesting.

"Nobody likes that gunk except for Justin," Ryan said.

"And I don't like it. I *looooove* it," Justin exclaimed. He grabbed a bagel chip, used it to scoop up a whole mess of the apple-chicken-liver dip, then shoved it into his mouth. "Yum!"

Then he spit a gob of half-chewed chip and dip onto the table. He grabbed a napkin and started frantically wiping off his tongue. "Burring! Waer!" he said, the words distorted by the napkin in his mouth.

Justin pulled the napkin out. "Water!" he shouted. "My mouth is burning. Someone tried to poison me!"

Motive + Opportunity

"We need to make him vomit!" Maddy shouted.

"No!" I barked. "Inducing vomiting is the correct procedure for only certain kinds of poison." I rushed over to Justin. "Open your mouth and let me take a look."

He did it without question. "His airway seems okay," I told Joe, who was already on Justin's other side.

"His pulse is okay too," Joe reported. "A little fast, but fine."

"It looks like he has a chemical burn on the inside of one cheek and on his tongue," I said. "We need to get poison control on the phone."

"I already called Syd," Rick said, just as Sydney flew into the room.

"Someone poisoned Justin! Don't let him die!" Kayla shrieked.

"I'm getting him to the hospital right now," Sydney stated. "You okay to walk to the elevator, J?"

"Yeah," Justin answered, sounding freaked.

I grabbed the bowl of chicken liver dip and handed it to Ryan. "Take this. They might need it to figure out what kind of poison he swallowed before they treat him."

"Right. Good," said Sydney. "Make sure everyone gets out of the room, okay?" she asked me.

"Of course." We all stared as Sydney hustled Justin and Ryan into the hall. "Let's all get our stuff together. We need to leave," I said when they were out of sight.

"I don't see why we couldn't stay awhile. Enjoy the flat-screen," Brian said.

"How can you be thinking about television?" Belinda demanded. "We don't even know if Justin's going to be okay."

"We should stay right here until someone comes and tells us how he is," Andrew said.

"Sydney wants us to leave," I reminded everyone.

"How did you two get to be BFFs with Justin Carraway anyway?" asked Brian.

I couldn't tell him we were on the Bayport High

welcoming committee. He knew there was no such thing.

"Our dad knows his manager," Joe answered.

"We'll let you all know how he is as soon as we know," I added.

Joe and I herded everybody out and onto the elevator. We followed them out the main doors, then doubled back to the guest lounge on the first floor. It was huge and pretty much empty, a good place to go over the case.

"So you think Elijah put the poison in the gross dip?" Joe asked.

"He doesn't like Justin. Maybe even hates him," I answered. "But if you were going to poison someone, would you let multiple witnesses see you bring the poisoned food into the room?"

"He was wearing a disguise," Joe reminded me.

"Yeah, but as soon as he picked up that camera, the disguise was blown. Elijah had to know that at least Justin and Ryan would ID him once he started taking pictures," I said.

"Good point." Joe nodded. "But the guy needs to stay on our suspect list."

"Definitely," I agreed.

SUSPECT PROFILE

Name: Elijah Gorman

<u>Hometown:</u> Scranton, Pennsylvania

<u>Physical description:</u> Age 27, 6'1", 215 lbs., light brown hair, scruffy beard, brown eyes.

<u>Occupation:</u> Photographer

<u>Background:</u> Single dad, with two daughters. Supports the family by selling photos of stars.

<u>Suspicious behavior:</u> Had a fight with Justin; had the opportunity to poison the dip.

<u>Suspected of:</u> Poisoning Justin.

<u>Possible motive:</u> Anger that Justin makes it almost impossible for Elijah to do his job.

I thought for a minute. "You know, the food was in the room for a while before Justin ate the dip. Long enough for somebody to add the poison."

"With the fight and the dancing and the poker, there would have been time for someone to add the poison without anyone noticing," Joe agreed.

"And Sydney is the one who uncovered all the dishes. She might have been able to slip something into the dip. She definitely knows it's Justin's fav."

"She was really angry with him tonight." Joe grabbed a cushion from the chair next to him and shoved it behind his head. "She basically said she had no life because of him. That's a motive for killing someone, right?"

SUSPECT PROFILE

<u>Name:</u> Sydney Lamb

<u>Hometown:</u> New York, New York

<u>Physical description:</u> Age 34, 5'7", 135 lbs., short brown hair, blue eyes, always wears gloves.

<u>Occupation:</u> Justin's publicist

<u>Background:</u> Has been working for Justin most of her career.

<u>Suspicious behavior:</u> Had a fight with Justin; had the opportunity to poison the dip.

<u>Suspected of:</u> Poisoning Justin.

<u>Possible motive:</u> Doing damage control for Justin is so time-consuming she has no life.

"She could quit," I said. "That's a lot less messy than killing him—and a lot less likely to land her in prison."

"People do stupid things when their emotions take over," Joe reasoned.

"True." You have to be logical when you're an ATAC agent. But a lot of the people we go after aren't logical at all.

"Talking about emotion . . ." Joe hesitated, then went on. "Emily got pretty emotional when I talked to her."

"She was furious at him during the shoot today," I said, remembering her and Justin going at it. With Elijah urging them on.

"She's hurt, too, though. And sad. She almost cried when she was telling me how she thought she and Justin had something real," Joe explained. "When he dumped her, it really crushed her."

"That's definitely one of the top motives for wanting to hurt somebody—a broken heart," I said. "You know what else is a top motive? Jealousy. I got to talk to Ryan for a while, and it's hard to believe he isn't jealous of Justin. I found out that Ryan didn't choose to stop acting. When that show they were on as kids ended, their manager decided it would be a lot harder to get both of them work as actors. They were too old to need to share a part at that point. So the manager, Slick, tapped Justin. He thought he had a better chance of success."

Joe let out a low whistle. "Harsh."

"Very harsh," I agreed. "And Ryan had the opportunity to put the poison in the dip. He also knows that dip is Justin's favorite."

"Even though Ryan is jealous, he also gets a lot out of having a star for a brother," Joe commented. "Justin bought him a car. Justin pays the bills for his credit cards. Justin dies . . . bye-bye meal ticket."

"But like we were saying, emotion can beat out logic." I stood up. "Let's swing by the kitchen, see if anybody saw anything unusual. Maybe somebody slipped the poison in the dip before Elijah even got his hands on the food cart."

We walked over to the hotel restaurant. "Two?" the hostess asked us.

"Actually, we just need to drop these off for my uncle," Joe said, pulling a set of keys—his—out of his pocket. "He just called and said he locked his keys in the car."

"I bet you're Tony's nephews. You kind of look like him," the hostess said.

"Right," Joe told her. "Uncle Tony."

"Go on back." She nodded toward the rear of the restaurant.

"That was too easy," I said to Joe as we headed for the kitchen.

"I'm so good I made it look easy, you mean," Joe said. He started to push open the double doors, then froze.

"What?" I asked.

"Just look," he answered, staring through the round window in one of the swinging doors. I moved over and looked through the window in the other.

Caro stood at one of the long counters, chopping celery. "She's really into being one of the Cleen Teens, and the CTs think Justin is a horrible influence."

"Working in the kitchen would make slipping some poison into Justin's special order pretty easy," Joe said.

"Let's not go in there right now." I moved away from the door. "I don't want to ask a lot of questions in front of Caro. If she is the perp, it would spook her."

"Can't think of anything else we need to do here then," Joe said.

I nodded. "Let's go home. Make a plan for tomorrow." I started back through the restaurant.

"My improvising worked pretty well today," Joe answered. "So I think I'll watch TV. But you plan if it makes you happy."

We took the elevator down a level to the hotel garage, still going over the pros and cons of planning versus inspiration.

"ATAC wouldn't have spent all that time training us if planning wasn't important," I told Joe as we walked toward our motorcycles. They were parked at the far end of the garage.

"We needed the training. I'm all for the training. But once you have the training, you—"

Joe stopped talking as one of the fluorescent lights overhead clicked off. Followed by another, then another, then another. Until the entire garage went dark.

I listened hard. I heard a slight scraping sound. Then, for the second time that night, the sound of breaking glass.

Thump

The sound had come from the northeast corner of the garage. Cautiously Frank and I moved in that direction. We stayed low, even though I doubted whoever was back there could see us. Not unless his—or her—night vision was a lot better than mine.

I picked up my pace. I didn't want to lose whoever that was. Frank stayed right next to me.

Up ahead I spotted . . . something. A darker section of darkness. I squinted. I thought it was a person.

I picked up the pace a little more. And then I heard footfalls moving away. Fast. Whoever was over there had bolted.

I charged after them, half bouncing off the bumper of an SUV. The thing was huge, but I still hadn't seen it.

Thump!

Sounded like the person I was after had slammed into something too. Good. I veered in the direction the *thump* had come from. The footfalls got louder. I was close, very close.

Suddenly I realized that now all I was hearing were my own sneakers slapping against the concrete. I froze. Where was the person I'd been chasing? Had he decided to hide because he'd realized he couldn't outrun me?

I turned in a slow circle, peering into the darkness around me. *Where are you?* I thought. *Where did you go?*

A current of air brushed against my face. Had someone just moved past? I took a step forward.

Pain blasted from my knees up and down my legs. I hit the cement hard. I tasted blood in my mouth as my teeth bit into my tongue.

Before I could shove myself to my feet, the lights clicked back on. Thanks to Frank. I jumped up and stared wildly around the garage. The only other person I saw was my brother.

"Are you okay?" he yelled.

"Yeah. Whoever that was slammed me behind

the knees with something that felt like a crowbar, but I'm okay."

"You're definitely in better shape than that car is." Frank pointed toward a sweet Lamborghini Murcielago—with broken headlights and a smashed-in windshield. Looked like it might have had a run-in with a crowbar too.

"Doesn't take a genius to figure out who owns it," Frank commented. "It's got a vanity license plate—STARCAR."

"You think somebody was upset they didn't actually kill Justin and decided to take it out on his Lamborghini?" I shook my head. "That's so wrong. That car is art on wheels."

"You sound more upset about what happened to the car than what happened to Justin," said Frank.

"The car is an innocent victim," I answered. "Justin, well, I like the guy, but he does have a few character flaws."

"So what's Justin really like?"

"I don't think I could have danced with him. My knees would have been shaking so bad I couldn't stand up."

"Is Justin as good-looking as he is in the movies? Is he really short? Tell me he's not really, really short."

All these questions and comments were directed at Belinda at school the next day during lunch. Because by lunch, everyone had seen the picture of her dancing with Justin in the paper.

"He's not short at all," Belinda answered. "Look at the picture." There were multiple copies laid out on the long table. Belinda kept getting asked to sign them. "Look how much taller he is than me. And he—"

"He's okay, right?" Andrew interrupted.

"He's fine. He didn't even have to stay in the hospital overnight," Belinda said.

Frank or I could have answered that. We were the ones who'd given Belinda the scoop. But the picture in the paper had made her the expert on all things Justin.

"I think that might be my arm in the picture," Chet volunteered, tapping an elbow that was almost out of the frame.

"No, that's Ryan. I remember he was over by us when the photographer whipped out his camera," Belinda said.

"Does Ryan still look exactly like Justin—like when they were little?" Sarah asked.

"Totally." Belinda brushed her hair away from her face. "But I didn't have any problem telling them apart. Justin . . . he glows, you know?"

Every girl around the table nodded. To me it was Belinda who had a shine about her. Her eyes were gleaming, and her cheeks were flushed.

"That's just on the outside," Caro said. She stood up from the table behind ours. "If you could see his personality or his morals, they definitely wouldn't be glowing. And Ryan's probably would. He's a lot better person than his brother. I bet if he was the star, he'd do some good in the world."

Frank elbowed me. And I knew why. Caro was sounding just like that stalker letter that had been delivered to the hotel. She was also sounding just like William Bost, but she'd probably gotten a lot of her theories from the Cleen Teens national president.

Caro turned back to her own table, and that's when I saw it. The black-and-blue splotch on the back of her calf.

Had she gotten that running from me in the garage last night? I remembered the *thump* I heard during the chase. Whoever had hit something hard enough to make that sound was probably working a big bruise.

Was it Caro?

Justin Time

"**W**imps! Wimps! Wimps!"

Our parrot, Playback, gave us his usual greeting when we walked into the kitchen after school. We didn't teach him that. Guess who did? Yeah, Brian Conrad.

"I didn't realize how late it was!" Aunt Trudy exclaimed. She sprang up from the kitchen table, whipping something behind her back. I'd caught a glimpse of it, and it looked like a hairbrush. Why was she acting so weird?

"Do you boys want a snack?" she asked. She backed toward the counter. "Maybe some pizza?"

Okay, now the weirdness was squared. Aunt Trudy might offer up some fruit or something when

Joe and I come home from school. But pizza? A few hours before dinner? No way.

"There's pizza?" Joe demanded. "I didn't know there was pizza." Joe always knows the location of any kind of snack food in our house.

"Um, no." Aunt Trudy struggled to slide open the drawer under the counter while still keeping her back—and whatever she'd hidden behind her back—to it. "But I could make some pizza. I know you love my homemade pizza! You go wash up, and I'll get started on it."

I had no words to describe the weirdness level now. Joe shot me an *I'm freaked by the freakiness* look. Had he seen the hairbrush? Why was Aunt T working so hard to hide a *hairbrush*?

Then I had a thought I really didn't want to have. At all. A hairbrush was one of the items that had been stolen from Justin's trailer yesterday. But there was no way Aunt Trudy would . . .

You've got to check it out, I told myself. *You can't get caught up in emotions. You're an ATAC agent. You see something that gives you any reason to be suspicious, you check it out.*

"I think you might have a fever, Aunt Trudy," I joked. "You know how Joe is. You make him homemade pizza for a snack today, he'll be expecting it every day."

I know—totally lame. But I couldn't think of anything else. My brain was on overload trying to store Aunt Trudy and suspect in the same file. I stepped up to her and put my hand on her head. Maybe I could see over her shoulder and—

She jumped away. And something clunked to the floor.

"I got it," Joe said.

He picked a hairbrush up from the floor. My stomach twisted. Now I could see silver initials on the back—J. C. "Those look like boar bristles," I said, hoping Joe would understand.

I knew he did when his eyes went wide with shock.

 JOE

Joe here. My eyes went wide with shock because Frank was thinking Aunt T could be Justin's stalker! I couldn't believe that he'd even have a second of doubt about Aunt T. She's the most honest person I've ever met.

 FRANK

Unlike you. You're so lying about your reaction. You thought the same thing I did. That's why your eyes practically fell out of your head. Now go. I'm telling this.

"Those aren't your initials, Aunt Trudy," I said.

She blushed. She dropped her gaze to the floor. She twisted her hands together nervously. Her body language was shouting, "I'm guilty. Guilty, guilty, guilty!"

"You boys aren't going to believe what I've done," she finally told us. "I never wanted anyone to find out." Then she went silent.

"What?" Joe asked gently when it seemed like she wasn't going to say any more.

"That belonged to Justin Carraway." She pointed at the brush. "I bought it." She threw her hands over her face. "I'm so embarrassed. I've behaved like a silly teenage girl, spending good money on something like that."

"You bought it?" I burst out, relief rushing through me.

"I know, I know!" Aunt Trudy cried. "It was a ridiculous thing to do."

"No, it wasn't," Joe told her.

"Lots of people collect celebrity memorabilia," I added.

"So many people were bidding on this." Aunt Trudy took the brush out of my hands. "Starlotta7 almost got it. But I was right there on the computer until the auction closed."

"You bought it online?" Joe said.

Aunt Trudy nodded. The redness was starting to fade from her face.

"Is there a lot of Justin Carraway memorabilia available?" I asked.

"There's a whole site devoted to it. That's all they sell," she answered.

"Show us," Joe urged.

"Joe's a big fan too," I added.

"Come on, then," Aunt T told us, sounding almost like her nonweird self. She led the way to the computer in the den, logged on, and quickly brought up a site called Justin Time.

My eyes immediately went to the words "New Justin Stuff" blinking in the upper right-hand corner. "Justin's pendant is for sale," Joe observed, just as I started reading the pendant's description on the screen. Stainless steel and teak. Rubber cord. Zen symbol. Just like the one stolen from the trailer.

"I think I've seen him wearing that pendant in pictures," Joe commented.

"I have," Aunt Trudy said quickly. She'd definitely forgotten about being embarrassed. "He must have several of them. This is the third I've seen listed for sale—and they are guaranteed to have been worn by Justin. Everything for sale is something he's actually used. His hair is actually still in the brush I bought."

"Hey, I have something for you, Aunt Trudy. Be right back." I hurried up to my room, grabbed the DVD autographed by Justin, and brought it down to her. "Joe and I and some people from school got to meet Justin because he's filming in Bayport. He gave us all these."

Aunt Trudy looked like Christmas and her birthday had happened on the same day. "This isn't supposed to be in the stores for two weeks!"

"You could probably make some money selling it online," Joe teased.

Aunt Trudy tightened her grip on the DVD. "I don't think so." She looked down at Justin's picture on the DVD case. "Charisma. That's what he has."

"Let's hit the homework," I said to Joe. I really didn't want to hear Aunt Trudy starting to talk about Justin's charisma. I'd had way too much Aunt T weirdness already.

We started out of the den, then Joe turned back. "So I'm guessing no homemade pizza?"

Aunt Trudy laughed. "I'll make you one tomorrow. For your dinner," she answered.

"You think the person stealing Justin's stuff is also his stalker?" Joe asked once we were up in my room.

"Why would you want the person whose things you're selling for cash dead? Dead people don't buy more stuff for you to steal," I reasoned.

"Although I bet the prices on the stuff that is available would go *waaay* up if Justin bit it." He pulled out his cell and hit a speed-dial number.

"Vijay?"

Joe nodded. "Vijay."

Vijay Patel works for ATAC. He's not a field agent, like Joe and me, although he wants to be one. But for now he's our go-to guy, especially on computer stuff.

"Vij," Joe said. "I need you to find out who is collecting the money from a site called Justin Time."

After he hung up, he immediately made another call. This time I didn't have a guess.

"Is this Ryan or Justin?" he asked. "You guys even sound alike."

By the time he hung up again, he'd made plans for us to take Justin and Ryan to the Bowl-O-Rama.

"You sure Bowl-O-Rama is a good place?" I said. "The lighting isn't exactly set up for stalker sightings." The bowling alley's claim to fame was a disco ball, laser lights, and old-school rock. It was pretty dark and noisy in there.

"Justin was itching to get out and have some fun," Joe answered. "He'd already heard of Bowl-O-Rama, and that's where he wanted to go. I told them we'd pick him, Ryan, and Rick up at the hotel in a couple of hours."

• • •

Sydney opened the door to Justin and Ryan's suite when we knocked. To me it looked like she was wearing a costume. She had on a skirt that looked kind of like a big bubble, a long jacket, and a pair of wrist-length blue gloves that matched her blue shoes.

Crazy, right? But it's not like I know anything about fashion. And she *was* from Hollywood.

"How do you two feel about Wi-Fi and anything you want from room service?" she greeted us.

"Syd, we're going out," Justin called. At least I thought it was Justin. They really did sound alike.

Sydney stepped back and let us into the room. "I'm worried about Justin going out tonight. Can't the four of you find something to do in here? Invite more people if you want. There's boxing on pay-per-view. You guys like boxing?"

"We're going out. She's just worried because I got another psycho letter," Justin explained.

Ryan appeared from his bedroom. "I think she has reason to be worried."

"Me three," said Rick from his seat on the sofa.

"I've gotten letters like that forever. What's the big deal?" Justin asked.

"The big deal is you've been getting more letters,

and this particular letter was creepier than usual," Sydney answered.

"The person who wrote the letter took credit for poisoning Justin last night," Ryan told us. "And for smashing up his car. When we got back from the hospital, his Lamborghini had a busted windshield and broken headlights."

Ryan thrust a piece of paper at his brother. "Read it again. And this time actually think when you read it."

Justin glanced at the letter. "It says right here that they don't want to kill me," he said.

"Can I see?" Joe asked.

"Sure." Justin seemed happy to get rid of the letter. Joe held it up so I could read it too.

Why haven't you learned? Learning is a sign of intelligence. So let's review, and see if it sinks in this time.

Your behavior is unacceptable. More than that. It's repulsive. You're a bad example to everyone around you. I saw you smash that reporter's camera yesterday. The man is trying to make a living. He doesn't have everything handed to him on a gold plate the way you do. And Emily. Can't you see how much you hurt her? Can't you see how much she's changed because of what you did?

I've seen. And that's why I decided to punish you. I knew that with all those people around you, someone would get you to a hospital in time to get your stomach pumped. And your car—it's just a thing. You have so many things, Justin. More than most people even dream of having.

I'm going to keep watching you. If you aren't able to learn from your punishments, then maybe you really shouldn't be allowed to keep influencing others to behave the way you do.

Be careful, Justin. Learn. I don't want to have to kill you.

"Clearly written by a nutball, am I right?" Justin asked.

"A nutball who found a way to poison you," Rick commented. "Maybe we should just hang here."

"We're going. At least I am," Justin announced.

"Okay, I get it. You're not going to listen to me or anyone else." Sydney let out a long sigh. "Take my SUV." She pulled her keys out of her purse and tossed them to Justin. "Maybe it will turn out to be a good thing if you go out in public. *If* you behave yourself. Let the person who wrote that letter see you acting in a way that makes it seem as if you've 'learned.' That might keep you safer in the long run."

"I'll be a good boy, I promise." Justin crossed his heart with one finger.

"You'd better," Sydney told him. "Otherwise you're going to end up a dead boy."

Battle at the Bowl-O-Rama

*F*rank was right. *This isn't going to be an easy place to keep Justin safe,* I thought as we walked into the Bowl-O-Rama. At least the place wasn't too crowded. A lot of people would have made monitoring the large space even more difficult.

We did the shoe exchange thing, then headed to our assigned lane. I kept my gaze moving, making sure to pause on every face. Almost everyone was staring at Justin. But staring at a big star doesn't make you a stalker, and I didn't spot anything that got my Spidey sense twanging.

The latest stalker letter had, though. It felt like the person who wrote it was getting more and more angry at Justin. And they'd moved on from just the letters. They'd definitely taken things up a level by poisoning the dip and smashing the sweet Lamborghini. They'd taken more risks. And that made them more dangerous.

But at the same time, that last letter sounded like the stalker really was more interested in changing Justin's behavior than hurting him. That moved Sydney up a little on the suspect list. It didn't make sense for her to kill a guy who paid her. But if she could scare Justin into settling down a little, she'd probably have time to hang in her hotel room and read a book. Have a life.

The new letter had specifically mentioned Justin's bad treatment of Elijah and Emily. That meant they should top the suspect list too.

Of course, the letter was telling Justin to do exactly what Cleen Teens wanted him to do—shape up and be a good influence on the world. That meant William and Caro had to stay at the top of the list.

Great. That made five suspects I thought should be at the top of the list. Frank and I should be able to wrap this up in no time.

Riiiight.

"You're up, Joe," Ryan told me.

I was distracted by the suspects battling for space

in my brain and by the fact that the stalker could already be in the bowling alley with us. But I still managed to turn the pins into a nice pile of dead wood. Just the kind of guy I am.

"Nice." Justin slapped my hand as I returned to my seat. I did another survey of the room. There were probably ten new people. Ten in the time it had taken me to knock down the pins.

"Always happens," said Rick, noticing my surprise. "I'm sure the second we walked in here, at least one person called a friend to tell them that Justin Carraway was in the house. Somebody else probably managed to get a shot on their camera phone and sent it to everybody on their contact list. And the paparazzi pay for tips on where Justin is. I'm sure a pack of them will be here within the next five minutes."

It didn't even take five. In three, Elijah strode through the door. In four, two other members of the paparazzi posse had joined him.

Justin didn't see them at first. He was dealing with a nasty seven-ten split. He took down the ten and almost put enough curve on the ball to hit the seven. But not quite. As he turned away from the lane, Ryan leaped to his feet.

"Some photographers are here," he told Justin in a low voice. "Elijah is one of them."

"Keep your rage button on mute," Rick advised.

"Repeat after me: good boy or dead boy." Ryan's eyes were intense as he looked at his brother.

"Good boy or dead boy," Justin muttered. Then he turned toward the photographers, grinned, and flung his arms out wide. "Who wants a picture of me in my bowling shoes?"

Multiple flashes went off in reply. "Maybe that will keep them off my back," Justin said when he turned back toward me, Frank, and Ryan.

I did another room check—and saw Belinda coming through the door. "This might make you happy," I told Justin. I nodded in her direction.

"Belinda, get over here!" Justin yelled. Like he'd invited her and he'd been watching the clock, waiting for her to show. The stalker thought Justin had a lot to learn. But he could also teach a thing or two about . . . I didn't even know what to call it. What had Aunt Trudy said? Charisma. Yeah, he could give a course in that.

"Did you invite her?" asked Frank.

"No," Justin said. "I don't usually have to do the inviting. I go where I'm going, and then I take my pick. There are always girls around."

"Around Justin," Ryan clarified.

"Oh, you don't do so bad, looking like me and all," Justin joked.

I was suddenly glad the bowling alley was so noisy. If Justin's stalker heard Justin talking like that, there would definitely be more badness heading in his direction.

"Hi!" Belinda cried as she joined us. I noticed she was all dressed up. I was almost sure the outfit was for Justin's benefit.

"Hey, gorgeous!" Justin gave her a hug, lifting her off her feet and swinging her around. The cameras went off again, but Justin didn't seem to care. "Get yourself a ball," he said when he put her down.

"Maybe that wasn't so smart," Ryan said when Belinda had left to choose her bowling ball. "The letter talked about how badly you treated Emily."

"I didn't do anything to Emily except decide that I didn't want her for my girlfriend," Justin countered.

"Yeah, but you—"

"I think my brother has a little crush on my ex," Justin interrupted.

"She's a good person, that's all," said Ryan.

Huh. If Ryan had a crush on Emily, that might give him a good motive to write that last letter. It mentioned Emily by name, even though, at least according to *Star Gazer*, Justin had treated a lot of girls kind of badly.

Belinda returned, and we all got back to business. Frank and I watched Justin's back while the rest of the group bowled. Not that I didn't continue massacring the pins.

Frank wasn't doing too shabby either. I watched him take aim at the single pin his first ball had left standing. He made his approach—

"Clean up your act, Carraway!" a girl screamed.

And Frank sent his ball right into the gutter. I jerked my head in the direction the scream had come from. The Cleen Teeners didn't have quite as good a communication network as the paparazzi did. But it wasn't bad. William—a smear of what I assumed was Goo Goo Cluster chocolate on his chin—Caro, and seven other CTs had arrived, signs and banners up.

I didn't like it. Way too many people from the suspect list were showing up.

Belinda's turn was next. "Justin, now that we have more company, why don't we blow this place?" Rick asked.

"Uh-uh. I have some things to see about first." Justin winked at a smokin' redheaded girl two lanes over. Then he walked over to her.

Belinda got a spare and launched into a cute little victory dance. Then she realized Justin wasn't around to take it in. "Where'd Justin—" She didn't finish her question. Didn't have to. She saw him for herself. Adjusting the angle of red-haired girl's bowling arm.

Flash, flash, flash.

Belinda stared for another moment, then turned and ran out of the bowling alley as fast as she could, dodging Justin fans, and paparazzi, and Cleen Teens as she went.

"I'm going over there," Ryan said. "It's like he's trying to get himself offed." He strode over to his brother.

"I think I'll go get us some beverages and tasty snacks," Rick told me and Frank. "Sometimes Justin is like a dog. You can distract him with food."

"That's not the only way he's like a dog," I commented.

Frank snorted. "True. Looks like Ryan's convinced him to come back over here," he added.

"All right. I'm back at our own lane," Justin said when they reached us. "Happy now, Mother?"

"No, I'm not happy now," Ryan snapped. "You're an idiot. An idiot with a death wish."

"You've just got your boxers in a bunch because I can walk over to any girl in the place and know, absolutely know, that she'll walk away from whoever she's with and whatever she's doing to spend time with me," Justin told him.

"That's not what this is about. It's not about girls," said Ryan.

"Not even precious, too-good-for-me-but-not-interested-in-you Emily?" Justin shot back.

"No. It's about you getting poisoned yesterday."
Ryan shook his head. "You were in the hospital last
night. The person who's after you—they aren't
fooling around."

"I can handle myself," Justin argued.

Ryan stared at him for a long moment. "Fine.
Whatever. Do what you want."

"I will," Justin said. "I don't need—"

"Got pizza," Rick interrupted. "And other neces-
sities." He started unloading snacks onto the plastic
chairs behind our lane. "Here." He handed Justin
one of the large cups of soda he'd brought back.

Justin took a swig, then spit the mouthful of soda out
on the floor. "That was Pepsi. You know I hate Pepsi."

"I said Coke when I ordered," Rick said.

"If you did, why did I just have Pepsi in my
mouth?" Justin demanded. Loudly. "Why do I even
bother letting you hang around me?" He swept
out his arm and knocked all the food and the other
sodas onto the floor.

Flash, flash, flash.

The paparazzi were on it.

"Get away from me!" Justin shouted at them. He
snatched up a bowling ball and heaved it in their
direction. It didn't even get close. Justin let out a
growl of frustration.

"This is what we're talking about!" William's voice rang through the bowling alley. He'd brought a megaphone with him. "Offensive, disgusting, repulsive behavior. His fans all over the world will see him acting this way—thanks to you." He pointed at the paparazzi. "And they'll think it's okay. They'll—"

"Would you just shut up?" Justin yelled. "This is my life. Mine."

"No, it isn't. You're a role model for millions of teens," William cried.

Justin grabbed another bowling ball off the closest rack—and charged at William. Bowling ball versus human flesh and bones. Not a contest I wanted to see. Justin could kill William if he smashed that ball into William's head.

I took off after Justin, Frank right behind me.

I managed to grab the back of Justin's shirt and jerked it as hard as I could. Justin stumbled back a step, and the bowling ball slipped off his fingers. He didn't bother to try and retrieve it. He yanked out of my grasp, strode up to William, and slammed his fist into William's face.

Caro let out a shriek of fury. She leaped on Justin's back, wrapping her arms around his neck.

Flash, flash, flash.

The paparazzi got busy.

I tried to pry Caro off of Justin. Out of the corner

of my eye, I saw one of the Cleen Teens smacking Elijah with a protest sign.

"Watch the camera!" Elijah shouted.

"You're a parasite! All of you. Don't you care what you're doing to the teens of America?" The CT smacked Elijah again.

And it was on. Total war between the Cleen Teens and the photographers. While Justin still fought to get to William.

Frank stepped between them and took a punch from William for his trouble. I gave Caro another tug, and she tumbled off Justin's back. Immediately she sprang to her feet.

"Get the car!" I called to Rick. "And Justin!" Rick waved to show he'd heard, dodging a chair thrown by the red-haired girl.

"Why didn't you get Justin what he wanted?" she shrieked.

She picked up another plastic chair. Rick dropped to his knees to avoid it, then started to crawl toward the door.

I grabbed one of Justin's arms. Frank grabbed the other. We each picked up a chair with our free hand and used them to clear a path through the war zone. We hustled him out the back.

"Get off me!" Justin yelled. "I'm not done in there!"

Rick pulled the SUV up beside us. Ryan slid

open the side door. Frank and I shoved Justin in, then jumped in next to him.

"Go!" I shouted to Rick.

"Justin, you are not to leave this room unless it's to go to work!" Sydney announced when we walked into Justin's suite. She had obviously already heard about the Bowl-O-Rama brawl.

Justin threw himself down in the closest recliner. "Who do you think you are?" he asked Syd. "You work for me. Maybe when I was three, I didn't know that. But I know now. I do what I want, and I'm going to keep on doing what I want. You don't like it—quit."

Sydney sank down on the sofa. Ryan sat down next to her. He had a nice black eye on the way. I didn't know if someone had hit him because they thought he was Justin or because they knew he was Ryan and didn't like the way he'd yelled at Justin.

"I'll got get some ice from the kitchen," said Rick. He looked eager to get away.

"Something's got to change, Justin," Sydney told him.

This should be a private conversation, I thought. But there was no way Frank and I could leave Justin alone. Not after he'd done everything he could to enrage his stalker.

I looked away, and something caught my attention. Part of the strip of light coming under the front door from the hall was blocked. I tensed. Somebody was right outside.

Justin's stalker?

Next Time It Will Be You

J oe nudged me and jerked his chin toward the door to the suite. I looked over and felt like someone had just run an ice-cold finger down my spine. An envelope was being pushed under the door. The stalker was right outside!

I bolted for the door, jerked it open, and rushed into the hall. Two steps away stood—Belinda. "Don't move!" I ordered her.

Joe snatched up the envelope, ripped it open, and began to read the letter inside aloud. "You tricked me. You made me feel special. But I'm just one of a million girls who love you. I know that now. What you did was so wrong. You deserve to die a slow and painful death, Justin Carraway."

Belinda tossed her hair back. She looked defiant and scared and sad all at the same time. "I'm not sorry I wrote it. I meant every word."

"You signed the letter," Joe said, stepping out into the hall with us. He handed it to me so I could look at it. Belinda's name was clearly written at the bottom, and the handwriting was different from the other letters.

"Of course I signed it," Belinda declared. She gave a harsh laugh. "If I didn't, he might never have figured out who sent it. He probably gets letters like this from girls all the time."

Justin joined us, leaving the door to the suite open. "Belinda, baby, you *are* special. Look at you," he said.

"So special you were practically making out with another girl right in front of me," Belinda snapped.

Justin laughed. "Come on, it wasn't like that. She asked me to help her with her approach. She was a fan. I didn't want to say no. I figured you wouldn't mind if I took a few minutes."

Sydney came out into the hall. "Are you insane, Justin? Are you actually flirting with your stalker?"

"She's not a stalker. She's a friend," said Justin. "She didn't write the other letters. If she did, she wouldn't have signed this one."

"What other letters?" Belinda asked.

Justin looked over at Sydney. "See?"

"Of course she's going to say that," Sydney told Justin.

Justin ignored her. "It's still early, Belinda. We can still hang. Let's go out. I heard about this club—Three Monkeys. It's supposed to rock."

Sydney opened her mouth. "Don't say anything," Justin warned her.

I had to say something. "Look, I agree Belinda didn't write the other letters," I told Justin. "But the person who did write the letters is out there. And if they know what happened at the bowling alley, they aren't going to be happy. I don't think it's safe for you to go out."

Ryan joined the big hallway group. "It's not. It's not safe, Justin."

Justin grinned at Belinda. "I'm going to go check out Three Monkeys. You coming?"

Belinda didn't hesitate. Didn't ask about the letters again. "Absolutely," she answered.

"You guys want to come, come. As long as you're coming to have fun, not babysit," Justin said. He leaned back into the suite. "Rick. You're coming, right? I need my Party King."

"I'm there." Rick stepped out into the hall.

Justin slapped him on the back. "Sorry. I had

trouble locating the mute button at the bowling alley. Coke, Pepsi, whatever. I'll drink camel spit if you serve it up."

Rick laughed. "I just might."

"Who else is in?" Justin asked.

"I'm staying. I guess I need to make some calls. Do some damage control," Sydney said. "How would you feel about doing something like a public service announcement? Might get a little goodwill going with that Cleen Teen group at least."

"Whatever you want. You're the pro. Best in the biz. And that's what I need, since I have so much trouble being a good boy," said Justin.

"I'm just going to say one more thing. Not as your publicist. As somebody who has known you most of your life. Someone who cares about you. *Be careful*." Sydney turned and headed toward her room.

"I'm still cute, right?" Justin yelled after her.

She looked over her shoulder at him. I could tell she was trying not to smile. "Yeah. So cute."

Justin was really good at turning people around when they were mad. If the stalker actually got close enough to talk to him, Justin might end up with a new buddy or girlfriend.

Not that I was planning on testing that theory.

● ● ●

"We get on the dance floor, and we all start dancing like monkeys," Justin said. "I want to hear some oohh-oohhs."

"First we have to get inside the club. With no ID. At least no ID that will help," I said.

"Don't worry about it," Justin told me. "You're in my posse now. Just give me one second." He trotted across the Three Monkeys parking lot and had a fast convo with the bouncer at the door.

Thirty seconds later we were inside. Dancing like monkeys. I wondered how long it would take for word to spread of Justin's location. Had the bouncer already made a call? Had one of the other people on the dance floor gotten off a text message? Did Justin's stalker already know where he was?

I glanced around the club. It wasn't any better than the bowling alley for keeping watch over Justin. It was even a little worse. At least the balcony was roped off for repair.

Joe danced his way over to me. He was getting into the monkey thing, scratching his pits. "We have suspect at four o'clock," he said.

I turned my head in that direction. The crowd was thick, so I didn't see her for a second. Then I spotted her. Emily.

She was moving toward us. Fast. Her face was twisted with anger.

Joe and I both automatically moved to put ourselves between Justin and Emily.

"Emily! Hi!" Joe called out. "Wanna dance?"

"More welcoming committee?" Emily asked him. "You're really devoted. Guess I'm not important enough to be taken out."

"That's not it. You—," Joe began.

Emily didn't let him finish. She strode past us and got right in Justin's face. Joe and I stayed close.

"I thought you dumped her." Emily jerked her head toward Belinda.

Justin kept dancing. "Belinda? No way. She's special to me."

Emily turned to Belinda. "Just so you know, there's somebody *special* everywhere we shoot."

"What do you care?" Justin asked. "You want me dead, right?"

"Right. Totally right." She shoved her way between Justin and Belinda, stumbling as she maneuvered through the crowd toward the door.

"Em, wait!" Ryan called. He hurried after her.

"She's just bitter because it didn't work out with us," Justin told Belinda. "Come on. Let's dance." He grabbed her and dropped her into a dramatic dip.

"I think you have to be a movie star to pull that move off," I said to Joe. Then I realized he was on his cell and had his finger plugging his other ear.

His eyebrows rose in surprise. "Okay, thanks," he said. "Frank and I are going to get something to drink," he called to Belinda, Justin, and Rick. "Anyone want anything?"

He got no's from all of them. "What's going on?" I asked when we reached a slightly quieter spot over by the coat check.

"That was Vijay. You're never going to guess what he found out about the Justin Time site," Joe told me. "It's owned by Justin."

"That makes no sense. Justin Time sells stolen stuff. If Justin wanted to sell memorabilia of his, he could just . . . sell it," I said.

"I know." Joe looked thoughtful.

I scanned the club as we talked, my gaze skipping back to Justin every few moments. I noted that Belinda wasn't dancing with him anymore, although four other girls were spinning around him. Which could be why Belinda wasn't dancing with him anymore. "Let's get back over there. Maybe we can find a chance to feel him out a little about the stolen stuff."

"We need to hit the bar for sodas first, since that was our excuse for cutting out." Joe led the way over. I kept doing my scan as he tried to flag down the bartender. I didn't see Emily or Ryan anywhere around. Maybe he'd caught up with her and they'd decided to talk outside.

Joe waved both arms over his head. The bartender didn't move toward him. But Justin spotted the motion and headed over. "Let me," he volunteered. He didn't have to signal at all. The bartender walked right over to him.

"That dude was here before me," Justin said, pointing his thumb at Joe.

"You didn't see Belinda go by, did you?" Justin asked as Joe ordered.

"Nope," I told him. "Think she's off writing another letter wishing you dead?"

Justin's brow furrowed. "Why would she be?"

"Uh, you started dancing with four other girls—at once," I reminded him.

"I didn't start dancing with them. They started dancing with me. And only after Belinda left," Justin answered. "She was just going to the bathroom."

"Probably a line," I said. "Hey, I meant to tell you. I was helping my aunt try to sell some stuff on eBay this afternoon. A couple of *Wizard of Oz* collectible plates. I couldn't believe how much movie memorabilia sells for. Do you keep anything from the movies you've been in—costumes or anything? You could make a fortune."

"I kind of already have," Justin answered.

"Oh. Yeah. Right," I said.

Joe returned with the drinks. "I have a sworn statement that this is Coke," he told Justin as he handed him one of the glasses. "I figured you might be thirsty by now. I'd be thirsty if I was dancing with four girls at a time."

Justin tried to suck down some soda through the tiny blue plastic straw in his drink. "It's like these things were designed for hummingbirds." He jerked the straw out of the soda, then grinned at me. "You want it?" he asked me.

I must have given him a "for what" look.

"To sell on eBay," he explained.

"I was telling Justin about Aunt Trudy selling her *Wizard of Oz* plates," I told Joe to bring him up to speed.

"You could make a ton of cash," Joe told Justin. "Every time you drink a soda, you save the straw. Ka-ching."

"Yeah, that's pretty much what I said. But I guess the acting thing is working out okay for Justin. He's managing to scrape by," I said.

"Maybe I should mention it to Ryan. I think he has a box of junk from *Five Times Five*." Justin took a swig of soda. "Not that he needs money either."

"It's pretty cool of you, buying him a Maserati and all that," I said. "If Joe became a millionaire, I'd be lucky to get a phone call."

"Don't say that, bro," Joe protested. "You know I'd call you on your birthday and Christmas. That's *two* calls a year."

Justin laughed, but then his expression turned serious. "What I give Ryan, it's not like a gift. I owe it to him."

That was worth following up on. "You've lost that many hands of poker?" I asked.

"It's just . . . we used to be one person, as far as business was concerned. If it was still like when we were kids, he'd be getting half of what I get paid for every movie," Justin answered. "He should still get *something*." He grinned. "Not half. I *am* the talented one. But something."

Justin drained his soda. "Why isn't Belinda back by now? How long does it take to go to the bathroom?"

"Girl bathroom time is like dog years," Joe told him. "For every one minute in guy bathroom time, it's seven minutes of girl bathroom time."

"That doesn't make any sense. A dog year doesn't actually last seven times longer than a human year," I told him.

"You see what I'm dealing with here?" Joe asked

Justin. "It's like living with Mr. Spock. That isn't logical, Captain."

"She has been gone a while," I said. What Joe calls his Spidey sense started humming inside me. "Maybe we should look around for her."

"I'll go back where we were, in case she looks for me there," said Justin.

"Try not to be dancing with more than four girls when we find her," Joe advised.

Justin gave a half salute and disappeared into the crowd.

"We may as well check the bathroom line first," I told Joe. "I think it's back that way, around the corner from the coat check."

The two of us hurried in that direction. As we passed by the main entrance, I saw Caro, William, and a couple of other Teen Cleaners. William flashed a card at the bouncer. A fake ID? That was so not Cleen.

The paparazzi couldn't be far behind, and unlike the CTs, they were old enough to get into the club with their actual IDs.

"This is definitely where the ladies' room is," Joe said when we rounded the corner. A line of at least ten women stretched down the hall. None of them was Belinda.

"Should we split up and do a search?" I asked.

"We haven't finished looking here," Joe answered. He walked to the head of the line. I followed him. "Will you lean in and yell the name Belinda?" he asked the woman closest to the door. "I'm worried my girlfriend is sick."

"Sure." She pushed the door open a little. "Is there a Belinda anywhere in there?" She got only no's. "Sorry," she told Joe. "Maybe outside. If I was sick, I'd want to get some air."

Joe and I decided to check the rest of the club before we moved on to the parking lot. We didn't spot her anywhere. "You don't think she'd have gone up to the balcony, do you?" I asked.

"Anyone could step over the rope blocking the stairs," said Joe. "I can't think of a reason she'd go up there, but we may as well check it out. We'll have a good view of the whole crowd from there. We can look for her and check on Justin, too."

We climbed up the stairs quickly. The balcony wasn't too wide, but it wrapped all the way around the club.

"Would it have killed them to have a little light up here?" Joe complained.

"No one is supposed to be up here," I reminded him.

"But they're using it for storage. There are boxes of booze all along that wall. Somebody has to come up here," Joe pointed out as we started around the loop. I followed him, peering into the darkness around us, then looking for Justin down on the dance floor. It wasn't hard to find him. He was in the center of the thickest part of the crowd.

I moved my attention back to the balcony, but not in time to realize that Joe had stopped cold. I stumbled into him. "Can you announce when you're going to do that? It's dark up here and—"

He stepped to the side. And I saw why he'd stopped. Belinda sat in a chair in front of us. Gagged. Hands tied behind her.

Carefully I pulled the duct tape off her mouth. She coughed and managed to spit out a wadded-up piece of paper.

Joe picked it up and moved closer to the balcony rail so he could read it in the dim light from the dance floor.

"What does it say?" I demanded.

"'Next time it will be you, not one of your girl-friends.'"

Panic! At the Disco

"Is she okay?" I asked Frank as soon as I finished reading the note that had been stuffed in Belinda's mouth.

"No bones broken," Frank said, running his hands down her arms. "No blood. I think she's in shock, though. What about Justin? Can you see him?"

I checked the bottom floor. "Got him. He's fine." He was picking plastic bananas off the fake tree by the bar, autographing them, and tossing them to fans. "I'll run downstairs and get Belinda some water. I don't think we want to try and move her yet." She looked dazed, her eyes unfocused.

"Good," said Frank.

I turned around and caught a flash of movement in the darkness on the other side of the balcony. "Someone's up here," I told Frank softly. "I'm on it. You stay with Belinda."

I locked eyes on the figure. It was heading toward the stairs. I wanted to catch whoever it was before they started down. If they made it into the crowd on the dance floor, I might lose them.

I put one hand on the balcony rail and ran, letting the railing guide me. *Gaining on you*, I thought. *Gaining on you*. I was on the same side of the balcony as the perp now. He or she veered toward the wall.

That wasn't going to help them any, unless there was a back set of stairs and the door was over there. I shifted directions too, moving away from the railing.

A small flame flickered in the darkness. I used it to guide me.

The flame exploded into a ball of fire.

Flying right toward me.

It smashed at my feet. Some paper stuffed into a bottle of vodka had been turned into a bomb. And another one was coming at me.

I dropped to the floor. Rolled. The bottle-bomb bounced off my elbow and spun away.

The smell of alcohol suddenly flooded me. Way too much alcohol than would have been in the two bottles. I heard a sloshing sound, and I got it. The perp was dousing the floor with booze now.

I scrambled to my feet. Before I could take a step, another firebomb flew through the air.

Whomp! It hit the floor, and a wall of flame sprang to life.

I could turn and run the other way. No fire behind me. But I would never catch the perp if I did.

I wasn't going to run away. I didn't care if I had to get barbecued to stop whoever it was.

I plunged through the flames. The smell of sulfur mixed with the overwhelming odor of the alcohol. It took me a second to recognize the scent. Burning hair. My hair was burning. I slapped at my head and kept running, racing toward the stairs.

I reached them. Empty.

I wasn't stopping. I took them two and three at a time.

"Fire!" someone yelled.

A couple of seconds later, a fire alarm began to pierce the music. "Please walk to the nearest exit," a voice said over the sound system. "Please don't panic. Walk to the nearest exit."

But it was too late. When I hit the ground floor, it was like being caught in a riptide made of people. Running, screaming, terrified people.

Someone slammed into my side, and I lost my balance. Before I could regain my footing, I got slammed again by someone else. And I was on the floor. Feet pounding by my face.

I started to push myself up, but a high heel dug into my back as a girl climbed over me, driving me back to the ground. Then a boot smashed into the side of my head.

The room spun.

And went black.

Where's Joe?

Where's Joe? That was my first thought after I got Belinda out of the building and into the parking lot.

There were tons of people milling around, but I managed to pick Justin and Ryan out of the crowd. They were standing together, a couple of photographers already snapping away. And good, Rick was right next to them.

But where was Joe?

I could hear a fire engine's siren in the distance. Coming closer. But not fast enough. Not if my brother was still inside the club.

"Joe!" I shouted. "Joe!"

He didn't answer. That didn't mean anything.

He easily might not have heard me. He could be out here shouting for me right now.

But I didn't see him. I didn't see him.

I knew the rules. You weren't ever supposed to go back into a burning building. People who did usually didn't come back out. But if Joe was in there—

"I need that!" I snatched a water bottle out of the limp hand of a girl standing near me. She was staring at the fire, transfixed. I'm not sure she'd even noticed what I'd done.

"Give me your coat!" I ordered the guy standing next to her. He handed it over immediately. I guess my voice told him I wasn't going to accept no as an answer.

I dumped the water from the bottle over the coat. There wasn't enough water to do more than dampen it a little. It would have to be enough. I threw the coat over my head and dashed toward the building.

"Frank, no!" Belinda cried out.

I didn't turn back. I raced inside. The smoke immediately seared my lungs and stung my eyes. I blinked rapidly, trying to clear my vision. "Joe!" I shouted.

He'd be low. He'd know to get down and crawl out to keep from sucking in too much smoke and passing out. I dropped to my hands and knees, searching the floor.

Over by the balcony stairs, I told myself. *That's where he'll be.*

That's if Joe had gotten down from the balcony. If he hadn't . . . there was nothing I could do. A section of the roof had already fallen in up there.

I wasn't giving any more thought to the possibility that he was trapped up there. He'd made it down. He had to have.

I crawled toward the staircase, an abandoned Cleen Teen sign sliding under my hand. My right foot knocked against something solid. I looked over my shoulder.

Joe!

I scrambled over to him and did a quick eval. Unconscious but breathing. I rolled him onto his back, then grabbed him by the shoulders. Keeping as low as I could, I dragged him toward the door. Picking him up would be bad. It was better to keep him on the ground, as far away from the smoke and toxins in the air as possible. As far away from the heat as possible. I knew the heat as little as six feet up could already be close to two hundred degrees.

Joe twitched and let out a moan, then started trying to lift his head. "Don't move! I'm getting you out of here."

I kept repeating those words in my head as I struggled toward the exit. *I'm getting you out of here. I'm getting you out of here.*

And we were out. Into the night air.

Ryan sprinted over to me. "Is he okay?"

"I think so, yeah," I answered.

"Let's get him into the SUV. We've already got Belinda loaded up," he told me.

"Good. Okay, good," I answered. We got Joe to his feet, supporting him between us. Slowly we made out way over to the SUV. Rick had the side door open, waiting for us.

Ryan and I loaded Joe inside, then climbed in ourselves. We joined the caravan of vehicles being directed out of the lot by the police.

"I didn't catch him," Joe muttered, half out of it.

"We will," I promised him.

"Catch who?" Rick asked.

I gave everyone a quick rundown of what had happened to Belinda. The threatening note. Joe thinking he saw the perp in the balcony and going after him. "I think the perp set the fire. To keep Joe from catching him—or her," I concluded.

"Whoa. That's like something out of one of your movies," Rick told Justin.

"Yeah," said Justin. I could see his face in the rearview mirror. It was drained of color. I think for the first time, Justin actually realized he was in danger. Real, non-movie, could-end-up-non-movie-dead danger.

"Is that dude okay?" Rick asked. "It looks like he's passed out in his car."

I looked out the window as we slowly drove by the parked car. "Stop for a minute," I told Justin. "Rick's right. He needs help."

Justin braked, and I jumped out of the SUV. The guy in the driver's seat was slumped over the steering wheel. "Maybe he managed to get to his car, then passed out from smoke inhalation," I suggested.

I tapped on the window. The driver didn't respond. So I opened the door.

The driver's body tilted, then slid out of the car and onto the asphalt.

"It's Elijah," Justin burst out.

He definitely wasn't a victim of smoke inhalation. Now that he was sprawled out on his back, I could see that the front of his shirt was soaked with blood. I carefully pushed the material up—and saw a deep stab wound.

Rick sucked in his breath with a hiss. "Is he—"

I pressed my fingers to the side of Elijah's neck. And felt nothing. No pulse. "Yeah," I answered. "He's dead."

Extremely Wrong

"So I guess Elijah's not a stalker suspect anymore," I said as Frank and I waited in the ER to make sure my head hadn't been permanently damaged or anything.

"I'm not sure," Frank answered.

"The guy's dead," I reminded him.

"I know. I was there." Frank rubbed his face with his fingers. "But maybe he *was* the stalker. He could have been murdered after he tied up Belinda and torched the place."

"Yeah, you're right. I hadn't thought of that. I hurt my thinker, remember?" I asked, tapping the place on the side of my head where I'd gotten booted.

"Elijah getting killed hurts my thinker," said

Frank. "Say he wasn't the stalker—the stalker wouldn't have killed him. Justin hates Elijah. Killing him doesn't hurt Justin. Not that Justin wanted the guy dead . . ."

"So we have a stalker *and* a murderer? We got two?" I asked.

"That's what it seems like. Unless the stalker had another reason to kill Elijah. Not as an attack on Justin. Something else." Frank stared down at the floor, thinking.

"Okay, say he was the stalker. Maybe somebody found out and killed him to protect Justin," I suggested. "Or, say he *wasn't* the stalker. Maybe Elijah saw the stalker do something suspicious. Maybe the stalker was worried Elijah could ID him—or her." I was pretty proud of myself for coming up with those ideas. My head hurt.

"I keep thinking about the fight at the bowling alley," Frank said. "The paparazzi and the Cleen Teeners got into it. The CTs really hate the paps for spreading stars' bad behavior around."

"Yeah," I agreed. "I guess they feel like if the paps weren't always catching teen stars like Justin doing non-cleen things, the stars wouldn't do as much damage. No as many people would know they were being bad boys and girls. So they wouldn't have as much power as negative role models."

"So we could have one perp. A perp who has something against Justin and the paparazzi," Frank concluded.

"I'd be happier if it did turn out to be one person," I said. "Otherwise we have somebody willing to torch a building *and* somebody willing to stab someone running around Bayport."

"One or two, the stakes got upped tonight. We've moved on from threats and warnings to arson and murder," Frank answered. "We've got to work this thing fast before somebody else ends up dead."

"Somebody like us, if we don't come up with a good cover story for what we've been doing tonight for Mom and Aunt Trudy," I said. "Doing a mission on home turf has complications."

Frank nodded. "Usually we can just say we're on a field trip or something and we're good for days. I don't know how we're going to explain the lump on your head—or this funky patch of hair."

I touched the little section of hair that had gotten singed. "Man, I'd almost forgotten about that."

"You know how we're always wanting Dad to treat us like regular agents?" asked Frank.

"Yeah."

"Let's trash that for tonight. We're going to need him to control Mom and Aunt T," Frank said.

"Good thing he's here then." He was rushing

through the waiting room toward us.

"I know that I'm supposed to treat you like I would anyone else," he said in a rush. "But I can't know you're in the hospital and not be here."

"Actually, we could use your help," I admitted. It hurt a little to say that. Not as much as my head hurt, though.

We settled on the story of a minor fender bender. I'd just stick a bandage over my piece of funky hair.

I wish the story had been true. Because in reality, our perp—or perps—had proven they were seriously out of control.

FRANK

Joe and I were on high alert the next day when we met up with Justin and Ryan in Justin's trailer. The director wanted some more takes of the scene where Justin got shot. That meant shooting in the crowd, with all our suspects in the vicinity.

The Cleen Teens—including Caro and William—were already out there, pressed up against the barriers, signs up. The paparazzi were in place too. Joe and I had seen them on the way in. Some seemed sad over Elijah's death. All of them seemed at least minorly freaked.

Emily was in her own trailer. Probably hating

Justin more than ever today, after seeing him with Belinda.

Sydney was at the other end of Justin's trailer on the phone with *Star Gazer*, telling them how heroic Justin had been the night before, helping get people out of the fire.

Ryan was right here. Sitting about two feet away from Justin. I had a hard time believing the guy would want his own brother dead. But it's not like people hadn't been murdered because of jealousy before. Lots of people.

There was a tap on the door, and my muscles tensed. The high-alert thing. Rick swung open the door. "They're ready for you, bro," he told Justin.

"The extra security is out there, right?" Justin asked. He'd really finally gotten that he was in life-threatening danger.

"All over the place," Rick assured him. "Almost as much security as fans, and that's saying somethin'."

Joe, Ryan, and I—and three security guards—walked Justin over to the section of Main Street that had been closed down for the shoot. He took his place next to Emily. When the director called, "Action," they kissed. No squabbling. Not tantrums. They just did their job and kissed.

Then Justin turned and walked away from her.

I did a suspect check, trying to lock each of their positions in my head.

"Stop!" the actor who was supposed to shoot Justin called out.

"I'm supposed to be the one who decides when to stop," the director told him. "What's the problem?"

"The handle of this gun is all sticky," he complained.

Instantly one of the crew members rushed over, cleaned the gun, and handed it back to him.

The director clapped her hands. "Okay, back into your starting places."

The clapboard got snapped together in front of Justin and Emily. They kissed.

My brain felt itchy. Something was wrong. There was something I'd missed.

Justin turned and walked away.

The gun handle is sticky, I thought. *Sticky*.

That was it!

I sprinted forward and hurled myself at the actor with the gun, taking us both down to the ground.

The gun went off. And the bullet made a hole in one of the cars parked on the street.

Justin sat down right where he'd been standing. He got it. He knew that he'd almost been killed.

The bullets in the gun weren't blanks.

"Get William!" I yelled to Joe.

 JOE

William bolted.

I bolted after him. The lump in my head protested with every step. The spot on my back that had gotten the high heel wasn't exactly happy either.

I put my hands on the low barrier and vaulted over it. Then I slammed my way through the crowd, elbows out. People had to get out of my way or get rammed. That's all there was to it.

I broke free of the mob. Which way had William gone? I looked right and left. There he was. Running east. He wasn't getting away from me. Not a second time.

I tore after him. William flung open the door of the Kiddie World shop. I was only a dozen steps behind him. I reached Kiddie World and pushed the door. Didn't open.

Through the big display window, I could see William shoving things against it. A crib. A freestanding closet painted with flowers. A dresser.

He wasn't keeping me out. I spun around. I needed something. Yeah. That would work. I grabbed the big metal mesh trash can on the side of the street. And I used it as a battering ram against the display window.

Metal versus glass. Metal won. The glass shattered. The trash can flew inside the shop. I followed it.

William was running again. I was right behind him. He knocked down a rack of baby clothes in my path. I jumped over it, ignoring the pain in my head and back.

I reached out and managed to grab the back of William's shirt. I had him. This time I had him.

The security guards swarmed the shop. Not in time to help or anything. But they did escort William back to the set for me.

"He's the one who substituted real bullets for the blanks," Frank told the guards.

"It was the sticky, right?" I asked. "That's what tipped it for you?"

"Yeah." He turned to William. "You should lay off the Goo Goo Clusters. You smeared chocolate on the handle of the gun when you made the bullet switch."

"I'm not the only one who eats chocolate," William protested.

But he was the only one of our suspects who could have provided the sticky. It couldn't be Caro— not the way she loved her hand sanitizer. Ryan was allergic to chocolate. I'd never seen Sydney without her gloves. And Emily didn't eat anything. She was on that liquid diet. There's no way she would have had chocolate on her hands.

"Why'd you run?" I asked. "If you didn't do anything, why'd you run?"

William blinked. "Because you were chasing me."

"Because you were guilty," Frank corrected. "You finally decided that Justin had to be taken out."

"We know you warned him first," I told William, deciding to play a little good cop. "We know you did everything you could to make him shape up and be a good role model for teens."

"But then last night you had a temper tantrum over getting the wrong soda!" William burst out, glaring at Justin. "And putting your hands all over every girl in the place. You knew what would happen. I told you. I told you I didn't want to kill you, but I would if I had to."

And . . . confession. That good-cop thing is sweet.

"And Elijah. Did you warn him?" Frank demanded, all bad cop.

"What do you mean?" William asked.

"You killed him, too. Because without the paparazzi, Justin wouldn't have as much influence as a role model," Frank said.

"I didn't kill him. I wouldn't kill anyone without a warning," William protested. "Justin got warnings.

The letters. The poisoned food. The smashed-up car." He turned to Justin again. "I didn't want to kill you. I tried everything else first."

I believed him. He was a psycho stalker. But he was a psycho stalker with his own honor code.

Which meant that whoever killed Elijah was still on the loose.

FRANK

"Well, we completed our mission," I said when we got home. We stood out on the lawn, wanting to go over everything before we went inside and had to act like your average middle-America teens again. "We found out who Justin's stalker was, and we stopped Justin from getting hurt."

"Yeah," Joe agreed. "But it's hard to feel good about it when there's still a murderer out there."

Aunt Trudy opened the door. "What are you doing out there, Joe?" she demanded. "I told you you needed rest. You were in a car accident yesterday, in case you've forgotten."

"I wouldn't mind a little rest myself," I admitted. We headed inside.

"We have something for you, Aunt T," I said. "We were watching Justin Carraway shoot one of his scenes today."

"And we got you a souvenir," Joe added.

"That does not make it okay that you went out," Aunt Trudy told him. But she couldn't keep herself from smiling a little as she held out her hand.

I put a bullet into it. "This is one of the blanks that was in the gun during the scene where Justin's character gets shot," I told her.

Well, it was one of the blanks that was *supposed* to be in the gun. When the cops had arrived, they'd found the box of blanks in William's pocket.

"You're good, thoughtful boys," Aunt Trudy said. "I've been thinking that you two should join that Cleen Teen group. You're exactly the kind of kids they're looking for."

 JOE

I lay in bed, staring up at the ceiling. It would be at least fifteen minutes before Aunt Trudy started threatening to pour water on my head to get me out of the rack.

Which was so unfair. I felt like I'd only fallen asleep about twenty minutes ago. I hadn't been able to get my brain to shut down. I kept thinking about Elijah. Who had—

My cell rang. I grabbed it off the nightstand. "Hello?"

"It's Rick."

He sounded a little distracted. Upset.

"What's up?" I asked.

"Justin's having a freak fit. He wants his Froot Loops, he wants new shoelaces—he hates it when those little plastic things at the end get cracked—he wants his hair trimmed and the hair person isn't here yet, he wants the episode of *Hell's Kitchen* he missed last week," Rick told me without pausing for breath.

I wasn't sure why he was telling me any of this.

"Usually Ryan helps me out with this stuff," Rick continued. "He's good at the brother management. But when I went into his room to get him, he wasn't in there. And his bed hadn't been slept in. If he was Justin, I'd say he just went out to find some fun last night and hadn't found his way home yet. That's exactly the kind of thing Justin would do. But not Ryan." Now I could hear a ripple of fear in his voice. "I think something might be wrong. Like, extremely wrong."

Here is a sneak peek at the next exciting book in the Double Danger Trilogy:

Double Down

FRANK

You probably think movie stars have it easy. Lots of money, loads of friends, 24/7 fun.

Well, okay, that's all true.

But there's a downside. Believe me. My brother Joe and I got to see that up close and personal this past week. We've been hanging with Justin Carraway. Yep. *The* Justin Carraway, Teen Movie Star. But before you get too impressed with our extreme coolness, we met Justin because of an ATAC case. See, Justin Carraway *does* have it all—including stalkers, loonies, and people wanting him dead.

That's where we came in. American Teens Against Crime—ATAC—asked us to become part of Justin's crew. He'd been getting a weirder brand of fan mail than usual. Not the usual "I love you so much, will you marry me?" type letters. These letters were threatening. And someone did try to off Justin. Turns out, a movie star can have as many enemies as he has fans.

Justin didn't exactly make it easy for us to protect him. That dude loves attention, likes to party, and doesn't want anyone telling him what he can and can't do. It's all about the fun to Justin. It took a dead paparazzo photographer and all of us nearly dying in a fire for the seriousness of the situation to register.

It was Justin's bad behavior that made him a target in the first place. The crazy letter writer was the president of a group called Cleen Teens, and they didn't approve of Justin's wild ways. Thought he was a bad influence on teens of America. I can't exactly argue with them on that point, but that doesn't give them the right to kill the guy!

Luckily, we figured out what was going on in time to keep the real bullets from being shot out of the prop gun—right into Justin's heart.

Something still nagged at me, though. That paparazzo. The Cleen Teen president—our perp—had no trouble confessing to his crimes. But he absolutely denied killing the photographer. Maybe he didn't want murder on his rap sheet; *attempted* murder was his limit. But still . . . the case didn't feel finished.

I just wasn't ready to let it go.

 JOE

Admit it, bro. You're not ready to let go of the perks that came with being in Justin's entourage.

 FRANK

That would be *you*, Joe. Yeah, sure, it was cool getting into clubs without standing in line, but—

 JOE

And the girls. Even *you* must have noticed the girls.

 FRANK

Just ignore him. I usually do.

Anyway, I was lying in bed, going over the events of the past few days, when Joe popped his head into my room, cell phone in hand.

"What's up?" I asked.

"Got a phone call," Joe said, flopping onto a chair. "From Rick Ortiz."

"The production assistant from Justin's film?" I asked. "What did he want?"

"Help."

I sat up, wide-awake and ready for action. "Was

Justin threatened again?" I *knew* we'd missed something when we couldn't tie the murder of the photographer to the Cleen Teen prez.

"Actually, it's Ryan," Joe said.

"Justin's brother?" Justin Carraway started in show biz as a double act—literally. Because of child labor laws, a child actor could only work very limited hours, so most TV shows and movies hired twins. One would work for a while, then the other would be swapped in. So Justin and Ryan shared the role of little Jimmy O'Hara on *Five Times Five,* an old sitcom. But as the Carraway twins got older, their longtime manager, John "Slick" Slickstein, decided that only one of them could become really successful. He decided that one was Justin.

Ryan seemed to be okay with it—he worked in his brother's company, and Justin was amazingly generous with the goodies. But still, it had to hurt to not be the chosen one. And to take orders from his own brother.

"Why does Rick need help with Ryan?" I asked.

"He can't find him," Joe replied. "Justin called Rick with his usual list of crazy requests. Rick went to Ryan's room to get some assistance, but he wasn't there. His bed hadn't even been slept in."

I frowned. "That's not like Ryan." Ryan was the responsible one in that pair.

"That's what has Rick worried."

"Do you think Ryan finally got fed up and split?" Ryan not only had to watch Justin make all kinds of messes, he had to clean them up, too. And it couldn't help that Ryan had a big crush on Emily Slater, Justin's costar. The same Emily Slater Justin had dated and dumped.

"Rick doesn't think so," Joe replied. "Ryan would have let him know. They're pretty tight."

"What did Justin say when Rick asked him about Ryan?"

"Rick hasn't told him yet," said Joe. "He was hoping maybe we knew something. Rick doesn't want to be the one to get Ryan in trouble."

I had a sudden thought. A disturbing one. "Could someone have snatched Ryan, thinking he was Justin? Those two are seriously identical."

Joe's blue eyes widened. "Oh man, I didn't think of that."

"If that's true, then Ryan is in serious danger," I said. "And Justin could be a target."

"We should get over there," Joe said. "The first twenty-four hours are crucial for clues."

We jumped into high gear. I grabbed the jeans and T-shirt I had worn yesterday and pulled on my high-tops before running out of my room.

I barreled down the hall and collided with Joe. He

was still yanking his T-shirt down over his head.

"Where's the fire?" our parrot Playback squawked from the armoire in the hall. "Where's the fire?"

"Shh," Joe told the parrot. "We don't want to stop for—"

"Breakfast, boys!" a voice called out from the kitchen.

My shoulders slumped. Aunt Trudy would never let us out of the house without a hearty—or as she jokes (lamely)—"*Hardy* breakfast."

"Can we sneak out the back?" Joe whispered.

"Where's the fire, boys?" screeched Playback. Loudly. "Where's the fire, boys?"

There are times when I think that bird wants the bad guys to win.

Just then Joe's cell phone rang again. "Rick," he announced, glancing at the phone screen. "Hey, Rick," he said into the phone. "Oh, okay. Well, that's good, then. Catch you later."

"Well?" I asked, after he flipped his phone shut.

"We can stay and have Aunt Trudy's waffles after all," he said, slipping his phone back into his pocket.

"Rick found Ryan?"

"No—he told Justin that Ryan was missing. Justin explained that Ryan went on vacation."

"Without a word to anyone?" I asked. That seemed out of character.

Joe shrugged. "Maybe Ryan didn't want anyone to talk him out of going."

"Rick would definitely have tried," I said. "Without Ryan around, he's going to have a hard time keeping Justin in check."

"No joke. He even asked if we'd be willing to keep hanging with Justin. Pitch in on the superstar errands."

"Maybe that would be a good idea," I said. "Not just to help Rick out, but—"

Now it was *my* cell phone that rang.

"My favorite all-American supercute good influence."

"Hi, Sydney," I said. Sydney Lamb was Justin's publicist. She was the one who set us up with Justin so we could find his stalker. That wasn't why she did it, of course—that was totally a secret mission. Our cover was that we were high school students (not a stretch—we *are* high school students) sent to welcome Justin to Bayport. She thought we'd provide "wholesome" photo ops for Justin, so she introduced us to him. She was always doing damage control, repairing Justin's bad-boy reputation.

Believe me, she earns every penny of her paycheck.

"So, I was wondering if you and your equally cute

brother would like to go with us when the movie moves to its next location."

"Really?" I asked. "Why?"

"Ryan took off without telling anyone," Sydney complained. "So not like him. That means other people—people like *me*—are going to have to pick up the slack. The biggest headache, of course, is keeping Justin in line. Maybe you and your brother can help me out there. I'd really love to have one day when I don't have to clean up some mess he's made all in the name of fun."

"I have a feeling that if Justin wants to do something, it will take more than Joe or me to hold him back."

Sydney sighed. "Don't I know it. But I don't know what else to do. We're moving to Atlantic City tomorrow, and there are just too many ways for him to get into trouble there. Rick will have *his* hands full without Ryan. And Justin already likes you. I can put it to him so it doesn't seem like you're there to babysit him. I can probably get you hired on as assistant PAs."

"Assistant production assistants?" I asked. "Does that job even exist?"

"It does if Justin wants it to."

"Let me run it by my brother and our parents."

"Great. Get back with good news ASAP."

I clicked off and told Joe about Sydney's request.

"Atlantic City?" Joe repeated. "Awesome! Cool casinos, fancy hotels, the beach, and all those perks that come with being around Justin. Of course we'll say yes!"

"Slow down," I said. "ATAC thinks the Justin Carraway case is closed. They could assign us something else."

Joe studied my face. "You don't believe the case is really finished, do you?"

I shook my head. "Nope. Not with a dead body unaccounted for."

"And ATAC isn't the big problem," Joe said.

"Mom and Aunt Trudy."

"Exactly. Gotta get permission."